CW00530049

SAVED BY GRACE

To Bob, Kim, Robbie, Parker, Steve, Kate and Adam.
With my love

You can have other words – chance, luck, coincidence, serendipity. I'll take grace.

(Mary Oliver)

Damien

Father Damien rinses his lunchtime plate and single knife and fork under the hot tap. He looks up hopefully at the kitchen clock – too early for whiskey. He boils the kettle and makes himself a strong cup of tea which he takes to his little verandah. There are two old sagging Parker Knoll chairs covered in faded calico and a pine coffee table on the shiny, red-floored *stoep*. On the table lies an open weathered Bible and a notepad. The sun is blazing through the torn blinds and the polished red floor looks as though it is melting in the shimmering heat. The only sounds punctuating the stillness are the ticking of the kitchen clock and the occasional rumble of a car's wheels on the dusty, potholed road in front of the simple little red brick house.

On the verandah wall is a collection of ageing framed photographs, some of them hanging crookedly out of their mounts. There's one of Father Damien with the walking group, leaning on a *knobkerrie*, his brown, muscular legs outlined against a pale grey rock, and another one of him and Cynthia in their bathing costumes, taken after they'd had a dip in a rock pool. He knows that Cynthia fancies him, as do a few of the other female parishioners, including Dorothy, the organist. In fact, Dorothy, with her thick ankles and huge spectacles is passionately in love with him. She makes excuses to practise the organ almost every day and, from the vestry, he watches her throw her buxom body at the instrument which thunders into a crescendo of sounds like a mini orchestra. Dorothy is always spent at the finale. Her face runs with perspiration, her mouse-brown hair clings to her head and her tortoise-shell spectacles are misty. Damien feels compassion for her but no affection. He wishes that she and newly-widowed, beige Malcolm, in his beige car coat, could find solace in each other's arms but Dorothy only has eyes for Father D. Perhaps it's the excitement of pursuing the unattainable, of loving a man she knows she can never have?

Cynthia had been the one to suggest a walking group and they'd ended up with six women and one male – Jerry, who wore long socks up to his knees, short shorts and a frayed cloth hat, and a hovering pair of binoculars poised around his neck like an extension of his body. 'Hell!' he'd exclaim, whisking the glasses with a sweeping stroke towards his eyes whenever he spotted an unusual bird, 'what a bloody marvellous sight!' Damien had felt a bit uncomfortble hiking with a band of women and had been relieved when Jerry had joined the group.

There'd been obvious jealousy among the women parishioners, jostling for Damien's attention (those whom the Italians refer to as *God's rivals*) but Father Damien has chosen this life of priesthood and celibacy and no other love must ever come between him and his God. It

4

should have brought him closer to God. But has it?

He takes a sip of tea and squints against the sun's glare. He can feel the sweat running down his back as he leans into the chair. His garden looks incongruous against the other gardens on either side of the little house. His lawn is green and he has hung flowering baskets from the branches of the acacia tree and planted hardy shrubs and geraniums in the beds he dug himself. Gardening has become his escape from the struggles and stresses of his life as a priest. He frowns at the sight of the bare barren yard next door, the dry red earth and patches of wilting mealies and the thin, mangy dog standing mournfully in the shade with its head hanging down and its teats dangling on the ground.

What was that poem he'd loved as a schoolboy? *The ground parched and cracked is like overbaked bread . . .* 1 How different is this harsh, brown African landscape to the moist green terrain of Ireland that he knew and loved so well? It had taken a while for him to get used to the hot, dry bushveld and the variety of brown, ochre and tan sepia tones, like monochrome photographs, and the rugged majestic granite rocks and hills. But after several months he had begun to breathe the air of Africa and had become a part of her unchanging, unhurried rhythm.

He closes his eyes and pictures the sprawling, impossibly green, fertile farmland and the wild beaches of his homeland; the village where he grew up, with its rows of brightly-coloured houses – red, orange, blue, yellow and pink – and the neighbours who knew each other well and were on first name terms with the postman and the milkman. You didn't need to lock your doors in that close-knit community and Damien had felt a soothing sense of belonging and protection, of shelter and security in the parental home.

At least that was how it had been before Da gassed himself in the VW when Damien was fourteen.

Mary

Mary Rose O'Mara pours herself a glass of wine, kicks off her shoes and settles onto the sofa beside her ginger cat, Rufus. She tucks her feet under her long cotton skirt and strokes Rufus gently, feeling the vibrations against her hand as he purrs contentedly. Rain is lashing in sheets against the window; she made it back home just in time. She takes a sip of wine and frowns at the pile of books waiting to be marked. 'They can wait till later, can't they, Rufie?' she says, as he kneeds her thigh.

It's been a long week, full of altercations between pubescent girls and meetings with concerned parents and Mary is looking forward to a quiet weekend. Perhaps she'll visit Maeve and Fearghus and have a good banter with her god son, young Damien. She sighs. How she loves that boy. He's the son she never had, the only tangible thing she has left of his uncle: beautiful, wise, gentle Damien, the only man she has ever loved. The man she was meant to marry.

She stares at the framed black and white photograph on the dresser: Mary, Maeve and Damien with their arms around each other, squinting into the camera lens. She and Maeve had just started wearing a bra and their little rose-bud breasts are outlined under their flimsy blouses. Damien has a faint dark shadow where his beard was starting to grow. The people in the photograph may have changed but the memory never does.

She closes her eyes and is transported back to those blissful years when she and Maeve and Damien used to lie under the oak tree by the stream and talk about the meaning of life; when Damien would help them with their homework and read them the poems that Miss O'Leary was teaching her English class. That was when Mary had discovered her own love for poetry: the sounds, images and emotions that were expressed in words that transported her to unimagined worlds. She can still hear Damien's deep, rich voice reciting:

I never saw so sweet a face
As that I stood before.
My heart has left its dwelling-place
And can return no more. 2

She'd felt as though her own heart had left its dwelling place when they'd taken that dare and jumped into the freezing stream and she'd seen Damien in his underwear. The muscles in his long arms and legs had glistened under the sun and little drops of moisture had run off his smooth, golden skin. His dark wet hair had clung to his face and he'd slicked it back with his fingers. She'd thought then that he was the most beautiful sight she'd ever seen. That was when she first saw him as a man and not as her big

8

brother. And when he kissed her after her seventeenth birthday party, she knew that she could never love anyone else but Damien.

And sometimes, when she's lying on her bed, the bed that had once been Ma and Daddy's, no matter how hard she tries to push the memories away, they still come sliding back into her mind and she remembers the smell of him, the sound of his voice and the sight of his fine, chiselled face. The way his dark grey eyes would flash with excitement and passion, and his hair would fall over his face when he was reading; the curve of his mouth and the perfect arch of his eyebrows. She grieves for what could have been, what should have been, and she feels betrayed and weeps. There was a time, long ago, when she used to know what he was thinking just by looking at his face. Now, the only thing she can rely on is her memory. Her memory never betrays her.

She finishes the last dregs of her wine and swings her legs off the sofa, then pads to the kitchen where she cuts a wedge of cheddar and eats it in front of the window. The driving rain has become a thin drizzle and the sky, through the misted glass, has a strange greenish tint. She gathers Rufus in her arms and makes her way up the stairs to her bedroom.

She runs herself a bath while she undresses in front of the long-length mirror of the mahogany Victorian *armoire*. Her soft cotton skirt slithers to the floor and she stares at her reflection. 'Not the body it was twenty years ago,' she murmurs, sliding her hands over her hips, her eyes scanning her shapely legs with their well-turned calves (courtesy of Daddy), her pale, translucent breasts which are losing their firmness, her thickening waist and her stomach which has a slight roundness to it. She sighs. *Life is passing you by, Mary O'Mara. What did Maeve's mammy used to say?* 'Me carriage has shifted.' She frowns as she pushes a tangle of dark curls from her face. When did those grey hairs suddenly appear?

Mammy used to swear by blackstrap molasses or onion juice to reverse the signs of greying (and a good dose of molasses was the perfect cure for constipation). She would apply a tablespoon of molasses to her scalp or rub in onion juice and leave it on for thirty minutes. (Not that it seemed to make any difference to Mammy's course reddish-grey hair, which she always wore in a thick plait wound around her head.)

Mary smiles at the memory of Maeve's Da coming home to the smell of raw onions and molasses. 'Och, Agnes,' he'd say, shaking his head, 'you been messin' with yer hair again? This house smells worse than a chippy.'

When she was a wee girl, waiting for Maeve before school, Damien would attempt to brush her hair. He'd battle to gather her unruly locks into a ponytail, holding the curls together with his left hand while his right hand tried to secure them with an elastic band. She'd shriek when he pulled too tight and he'd frown and mutter. 'Will you wind yer neck in, Mary? Hold still now, while I finish!' What other adolescent boy would have risked being mocked and teased for brushing a little girl's hair? But Damien was always so self-assured and unconcerned about what other people thought.

Ah, Father Damien, she thinks, wistfully, *you must surely be the most perfect priest.*

She climbs into bed with Rufus curled up beside her and reaches for her book on the nightstand.

Damien

Damien had been walking his ten-year-old sister, Maeve, and her best friend, Mary, home from school just before he'd found Da. Mary's unruly locks had escaped the elastic band again and loose tendrils were trailing down her neck. 'Will you look at the state o' you, Mary?' he'd teased, 'sure, yer hair is a right mess now!'

Mary and Maeve had giggled and swung their satchels at him.

'Ah, don't you pups be actin' the maggot now! G'wan and wash yer hands. Mammy's waitin' to wet the tea.'

Mary's mother had died when she was four and Mammy had taken her under her wing, looking after her during the day until her father, Frank, got home from his work at the dairy. Damien had become like a big brother to her and believed that he could protect and shield her from anymore of life's cruel blows. He'd taught her how to buckle her shoes and brush her thick, black, curly hair that looked midnight-blue when the sun shone on it. Unruly tendrils would always escape and curl around the nape of her neck and the little hollow at its base that made her seem so vulnerable to Damien. Her huge eyes, encircled by thick black lashes, were bluer than any blue he had ever seen. They were like the china-blue glass eyes of Maeve's doll, Adelaide, with her long painted eyelashes and one eyelid that closed whenever Maeve turned her upside down to

12

make her cry – which was often. She and Mary had never really been interested in dolls and Adelaide's leg had finally broken off, after years of being lugged around by her foot. She'd been relegated to the toy box alongside Raggedy Ann, with her red hair and face like a scarecrow, and Surgeon Barbie with her face mask and bright blue eyeshadow. Her stethescope had ended up being wound around Adelaide's neck.

Mary had a habit of pressing her lips together when she was concentrating and two little dimples would appear on either side of her mouth. She'd breathe heavily and sigh as she tried to tame her curls before throwing down the brush in frustration. 'Dami, will you do it?' she'd ask, her cheeks flushed with vexation. He'd gather her locks together, then put his hands on her shoulders and look her up and down. The hem of her oversized uniform hung below her knees and her little pigeon-toed feet were clad in white bobby socks and black Mary-Jane shoes. 'Look at you there now, Mary Rose,' he'd say, 'so neat and pretty you are.'

She'd giggle and look away, embarrassed.

'Two little shitehawks, so they are,' said Mammy. 'By the end of the day they'll both be a right mess.'

Miss O'Leary

The day that Damien found Da, Miss O'Leary had been teaching them a new poem called Storm at Sea.

Prepare yourself for life's cruel blows,
For shipwreck and for storm,
There is a light within you,
It's there since you were born. 3

She had explained that the storms of life were traumas, deaths, illnesses, betrayals, abandonments and injustices. 'Tis a foolish man who tinks dat his own strength, courage and determination will be enough to see him troo,' she'd said earnestly, blinking her sad, pale-blue eyes. She always smelt of lavender and had a little lace handkerchief clasped in her right hand. She pronounced poetry, *poo-etry.*

It was rumoured that Miss O'Leary had been disappointed in love when she was in her early twenties and working as a barmaid at McGinty's in Dublin. She had just finished her shift with pretty, buxom, blonde-haired Nancy Roarke when Mr McGinty had given her a note from a male customer. In it was written, in neat cursive, the name, *Hugo Fothergill*, with an address in Paris.

Miss O'Leary had been curious and had written to Mr Fothergill and that had been the start of a correspondence spanning a year. They had discovered that they both had much in common: a mutual love of literature and poetry

14

and of music and theatre. Finally, the day had arrived when Mr Fothergill would be visiting Dublin again. Miss O'Leary had dressed carefully for their meeting and had pinned her mousey brown hair into a French roll and lavishly applied Yardley's English Lavender behind her ears and on her wrists. They'd arranged to meet in a coffee shop and Mr Fothergill said that he would be wearing a red rose in his lapel. He was already sitting at a corner table next to a rubber plant when she arrived and she'd walked up to him, smiling shyly. He'd looked up at her eagerly and the smile on his face had frozen. He'd stood up, shaking his head, and had then uttered those devastating, fatal, heart-breaking words: 'You're the wrong woman.' His note had been intended for Nancy.

Damien didn't really understand what betrayals and abandonments meant but he did believe that he could protect Mary from the pain of her mammy's death.

Until he'd found Da slumped lifeless over the steering wheel.

From that moment on, he had been in a constant state of emotional pain and when he occasionally allowed himself to revisit his grief, it was still as poignant and crippling as it was that day. Somehow they had just muddled through it, with Mammy's face frozen into a false smile and Maeve's pale face wide-eyed and questioning. They never spoke about Da again

15

and had borne the whispering and pointing with silent stoicism. Damien had realised then, at the age of fourteen, that he hadn't been able to prepare himself for life's cruel blows and that he would have to search for 'the light within'.

He'd found odd jobs to do after school, like helping Mr Patel at his shop, and had worked at the bookshop at the weekends to help Mammy put food on the table. Seamus Rafferty had become his best friend because he too had lost his father and understood the depression and despair that Damien felt. But, when Seamus was sixteen, he began to binge drink and indulge in casual sex and drugs and he and Damien had drifted apart.

'Look at the state o' you, Seamus! Would you ever catch yerself on and wise up, man?' Damien would say, exasperated, 'sure yer actin' like a feckin' eejit now!'

'Ah, now, Damien,' Seamus would reply, angrily, 'get over yerself, man. Yer startin' to become a feckin' dryshite. I like bein' pissed. There's more to life than books and yer feckin' poetry.'

Seamus didn't know that Damien had secretly started writing his own poetry. He had only shown it to Miss O'Leary and she had urged him to continue writing. 'Da pain you feel now, Damien, son, can be transformed into somethin' beautiful, if you'll let it,' she'd said, looking into his eyes with deep compassion and empathy.

He hadn't even shown his poems to Maeve or Mary because he didn't want them to guess how sad and unhappy he really was and how much he missed Da.

But Miss O'Leary knew.

Maeve

Maeve makes herself a cup of coffee and takes it up to her study where she settles herself behind the computer. The house is quiet, now that the boys and Fearghus have gone for a run. She waits for her e-mails to appear on the screen and glances idly at the framed photographs on the bookcase. There's one of her beloved golden retriever, Dottie, who had had to be euthanased a year ago after the pain from her hip dysplasia had become unbearable. The pain of Maeve's grief over the loss of her friendly, high-spirited companion, with her sweet face and waddling gait, had also been unbearable at first and she's been loathe to replace her dog ever since. After they'd buried her under the chestnut tree, she'd written a poem about Dottie and tucked it behind the photograph in the frame. Brendan had made a headstone from a flat piece of slate and painted in clumsy script, *Dottie – Forever loved and missed.* The wet paint had dripped in white streaks under the words, so that they spelled *Pottie.*

There's a picture of her and Fearghus with the boys, standing proudly beside a newly-ordained Father Damien in his black robe and dog collar, and one of her and Fearghus laughing at the church door after their wedding. Her head is thrown back and her arms are flung out, with one hand clutching her bouquet. There's another one of little Damien and Brendan playing on the beach and one of Mammy and Da when they were young, Da in his flat cap and Mammy with her plaited hair wound around her head.

She takes a picture from the bookcase and blows a film of dust off its surface. Maeve, Mary and Damien are laughing into the camera with their tennis racquets raised triumphantly in the air, after a sweaty game of doubles with Seamus Rafferty. He'd never even seen a tennis racquet before then and had been mortified when he'd been unable to return Damien's powerful serve. Maeve smiles with satisfaction, remembering him throwing his racquet down angrily, muttering, 'Feck this, man! I'm knackered.' *Why, in God's name, did Mary marry that tool?* she thinks, frowning.

Everyone had thought that Mary and Damien would marry when he had finished his degree. They just seemed to belong together, as though they were one soul in two bodies. Mary would refuse to talk about it, would never give an explanation, and Maeve had given up trying to find an answer. It wasn't like she was pregnant and had to marry Seamus and she knew what a chancer he was. No one was surprised when she booted him out after years of putting up with his philandering with Rosheen Murphy – oh, yes, Maeve herself had been a witness to that. Mary and Damien would have made a perfect couple and Damien would not have sacrificed himself to the church. Didn't Mary know what her betrayal had done to him, how she had ripped his heart to shreds?

Maeve brushes away a tear and scrolls through her e-mails. There's one from Father Farwell, asking for Damien's contact details – the Christian Brother's College is having a reunion. She hesitates before she replies. A reunion. Could Damien be persuaded to come home? She hasn't seen him for six years, not since she and Fearghus took the boys to Africa and stayed in that hot little red brick house that her brother called home. She'd been surprised at how healthy Damien had looked, his lean body tanned and strong. He'd always had a dark complexion and the harsh African sun had burned it golden-brown. His hair was greying at the temples, which Maeve had thought made him look distinguished, and he had some deep furrows across his forehead, but he was still that perfect specimen of manhood that she had always admired and, of course, the women in his parish idolised him. Especially that poor lumbering organist. *What was her name again? Dorothy.*

Maeve runs her fingers through her mop of curly golden hair. It's starting to look like Mammy's wiry reddish-brown hair before it started to go grey. She winces as she remembers the smell of molasses and onion juice and Da's reaction to the foul stench when he came home.

Why are men considered distinguished when their hair goes grey but women just look old?

They hadn't talked about Mary during that holiday in Africa, other than the fact that she and Seamus were divorced, but Maeve had seen the deep sadness creep into her brother's eyes before he had abruptly changed the subject.

That familiar yearning to see her brother again wells up inside her and she resolves that she will write to him now and try to persuade him to come home for the reunion.

Damien

Mary and Maeve had been glued at the hip throughout their teenage years and Damien still watched over them jealously. In the long summers they would ride their bikes along the country lanes and pick apples and blackberries, which they'd eat whilst lying against the roots of an old oak tree next to a stream, their lips stained purple. They'd talk about the meaning of life and what happens when you die but they could never bring themselves to ask the question about whether or not Da had gone to heaven. Damien taught the girls to play stone-skipping and they'd have competitions to see how many times their stones would skip over the smooth, glassy surface of the stream before sinking. Sometimes they'd play silly guessing games and would ask each other what they'd like to be one day.

'What kinda animal would you choose to be?' Maeve had asked, biting into an apple, her golden hair trailing against her face.

'A cat,' Mary had said, without hesitation, 'a ginger cat with green eyes.'

Damien had thought for a while, before replying. 'An elephant.'

'I'd be a dog,' said Maeve, 'a golden Labrador.'

On one unusually sunny day they took a dare and jumped into the freezing stream in their underwear. Damien's heart had stopped at the sight of Mary in her white cotton bra and knickers with little embroidered daisies; her flat stomach and firm round breasts, with their nipples outlined against the wet fabric, and her gently curving waist. At that moment he knew that he was now a man and she was a woman and one day he was going to marry her. And afterwards, lying on his bed, unable to sleep, he'd remembered the words of John Clare, the poet they were studying at school.

I ne'er was struck before that hour
With love so sudden and so sweet,
Her face it bloomed like a sweet flower
And stole my heart away complete. 4

To Mammy's delight, he'd won a scholarship to Trinity College in Dublin while Maeve and Mary had continued with their O Levels at Holy Cross Convent. He would come home for his breaks and spend the days studying, cycling and swimming (when it wasn't raining) with Maeve and Mary. He'd helped them with their own studies, talking earnestly long into the night, and would read his favourite poetry to them under the oak tree: Louis Macneice, W B Yeats, T S Eliot and Mary Oliver. 'She always kept her eyes peeled for animals,' he told them, 'and they appeared like kindred spirits in her poems.'

'Did she write poems about dogs?' asked Maeve, her wet golden hair hanging down her face like droopy dog ears.

'She did too,' Damien said, *'Dog Songs.'*

After he had returned to university, Maeve and Mary would read the poems together, lying on their stomachs on Maeve's bed.

> *I had a dog*
> *who loved flowers.*
> *Briskly she went through the fields . . .* 5

Somehow, just reading the poems together had made Damien's absence feel less painful. Mary didn't tell Maeve, but she missed him terribly and ached for his presence, counting the days until his return. He didn't frequent the pubs and clubs like Seamus did and was content just to be with Mary. Sometimes their hands would brush or her fingers would linger on his arm for a moment and he'd feel a thrill of excitement. He didn't know if she felt the same love and desire that he felt until the night of her seventeenth birthday.

Her father had organised a party for her at the town hall, with a buffet supper and a local band in attendance. Damien had just arrived at her house, bearing a carefully-wrapped gift of *The Selected Poems of W B Yeats*, as Mary was descending the staircase. She was wearing a crimson strapless dress, her shiny black hair flowing over her shoulders, and her lips were stained a deep cherry-red. He had felt like Rhett

24

Butler looking up at Scarlett O'Hara and had been mesmerised by her beauty. They had danced together all night, rounding off the evening doing silly jigs and reels and when the party had ended, Damien had walked her home. Under the dim porch light he had kissed her and he can still recall the feel of her soft lips and her smooth creamy skin. He had run his fingers through her lustrous black hair and breathed the smell of fresh flowers and apples and he'd wanted that moment to last forever. 'Ah, Mary Rose O'Mara,' he'd whispered, 'you have stolen my heart. Tread softly because you tread on my dreams.' 6

He knew then that he loved her more than anything else in the world and would love her for the rest of his life.

Damien

Which was why his heart had been shattered into a million pieces when Mammy had written to say that Mary was about to marry Seamus Rafferty.

For the life of us, Damien, she wrote, *we cannot fathom why she would choose a snake like Seamus. She's wasted on him, son. Poor Frank is dying and his heart is broken . . .*

It was then that Damien understood what Miss O'Leary had meant by abandonment and betrayal. Didn't Mary know that he was waiting for her to finish her studies, to complete his degree and get a good job, so that he could offer her a future? How could she, then, have given herself to Seamus? Everything that Damien had ever believed about himself and about love had been ripped to shreds and the pain he'd felt in his tortured mind was almost physical. He never went home again, until he'd heard that Seamus and Mary had moved away. By then, Maeve had married Fearghus McCarthy and had given birth to two little boys, Damien and Brendan.

Mammy had always wanted her son to enter the priesthood and at the age of twenty-eight he had been ordained. If he couldn't have Mary O'Mara, God could have him. If he couldn't be married to Mary, he'd be married to the church. He would be an instrument of the Lord, the perfect priest with an undivided heart, the conduit between God and man; and over the years he had taught himself to sublimate his passions.

The mystical significance of the church rituals, the Latin cadences and the incense, the stained glass windows and the lace and gold embroidery had never really excited him. He had no ambitions to rise through the ranks or to become a cardinal; he didn't even aspire to become a bishop. He was content celebrating Mass, comforting the lonely, the sick and the dying and performing marriages and funerals. Hearing confessions had soon become tedious and he'd often found himself nodding off before assigning penance: 'Say three *Hail Mary's*, two *Our Fathers* . . . ' The sins of the elderly were generally predictable: 'Bless me, Father, for I have sinned . . . I broke a promise, I fell asleep during Mass, I was impatient or jealous.' The sins of the young people (when they did attend Mass) were mostly of a sexual nature and Damien felt ill-equipped to offer advice or penance. *The perfect priest*, he would think, contemptuously. *I am not a priest; I am not even a man.*

When he had entered the seminary, Mammy had given him Da's Bible. 'Tis as good as new, son,' she'd said, 'never been read.' One lonely night he opened it and discovered a Letter of

Demand tucked between the pages. His eyes had scanned the words in front of him:

Unless full payment of the outstanding amount is made by . . . I shall commence legal proceedings to recover the debt . . . this letter will be tendered in court as evidence of your failure to pay.

'Oh Da!' he had cried, tears pouring down his face, 'if only we'd known. Was it worth yer life, man? Was it worth yer life?' He'd wept bitterly for his poor, helpless father who could see no way out and for his mammy who'd been the butt of village gossip for months afterwards. He'd eventually shown the letter to Maeve and they'd both agreed not to tell Mammy. She'd already lived with enough shame.

Following his ordination he'd been assigned as associate pastor to a small parish in the country, after which he'd been appointed parochial vicar at a parish in County Clare, before accepting the assignment to Africa. Perhaps a new start in a new country would help him to forget Mary O'Mara and to focus on God's work?

One week after he arrived in the dusty little town, Mammy passed away peacefully in her sleep.

Da

Damien and Da had always shared a close relationship and Damien's dream was to be just like him. Dear kind, good-natured Da, so different to the fathers of his friends who spent hours in the pub, wasting their wages, coming home smelling of Guiness and singing bawdy songs. Da was honourable and wise and he'd taught Damien that integrity was all that really mattered. 'Tis the only virtue you need, Damien, son. Tis doin' the right thing, even if nobody knows that you did it. If you have it, nothin' else matters; if you don't have it – well, nothin' else matters.'

He would often quote the Danish philosopher, Soren Kierkegaard, recounting to Damien his search to understand himself before he could know anything else, including God. 'He looked to philosophy as a way to escape religion until he had his own spiritual experience which he described as a feelin' of indescribable joy. That was when he finally understood that he was a person, found by God. He wrote many books which you can read when you're older, son. The first one was called *Either/Or.'* Da had sucked on his pipe for a few minutes and had then quoted, softly, 'faith is either God, or – well, the rest doesn't matter.'

He used to smell of pipe tobacco and *Brylcreem* and Damien would sometimes take a dab of hair cream from the red and white tub in Da's bathroom cabinet and run it through his own hair to smoothe it down. He loved watching Da carefully packing tobacco into the bowl of his pipe before there'd be the *whoosh!* of the match. Da would move it over the tobacco surface, taking small puffs, until the familiar aromatic smell would fill the room and he'd be engulfed in a cloud of smoke.

After he'd died, Damien quietly removed Da's pipe from the little oak table next to his chair in front of the fire and wrapped it in one of his handkerchiefs. He'd kept it hidden at the back of a drawer until he couldn't bear the pain anymore of smelling Da every time he opened the drawer. So, he moved it to an old tin box in which he kept special things like a hardening conker, a 1982 one penny coin, a VW matchbox car like Da's, an elastic hair band which had belonged to Mary, some of his own secret poems and Da's cassette tapes. The box lid depicted *The Landing of Bonnie Prince Charlie at Eriskay* and had a dent in the side and some slight paint loss. Da had discovered it at *Martin Fennelly Antiques* in Dublin and gave it to Damien when he was twelve. 'Keep it safe, lad,' he'd said, tapping his pipe bowl against the ashtray, 'it's very valuable; it's an antique.'

Da didn't use the VW much, except to take Mammy to do her monthly shop at Tesco or for trips to the beach. They didn't go to the beach often because it would usually be raining at the weekends, but Damien does remember one particular trip when Mammy had packed a picnic and they'd loaded the VW with deck chairs and towels and an umbrella. They'd chugged along behind a huge lorry which Da couldn't overtake, while the blue sky had been slowly turning an ominous shade of grey.

'Sure, tis fierce windy out, Albert,' Mammy had said, anxiously, as the little car swayed behind the lorry, 'looks like rain. Soon be bucketin' down, so it will.'

Da had held onto the steering wheel grimly, refusing to acknowledge that it was not going to be the perfect day for the beach. 'Och, Agnes,' he'd said, frowning, 'wind yer neck in. Tis only spittin'.'

When they'd arrived at the beach, the wind was howling and the waves were crashing but they'd doggedly laid out their towels and the picnic basket. Mammy was wearing a bathing suit with a little skirt around her thighs and it was flapping in the wind. 'Me hair's all over the shop, Albert!' she'd complained, trying to hold onto her hair and the little skirt at the same time, 'I'll be blown to smithereens, so I will!' Her thighs were white and dimpled and reminded

31

Damien of the cottage cheese she used to make after it had been strained through cheesecloth. She would add the leftover whey ('waste not, want not') to soups and stews and had once poured it over her hair before shampooing it because Fatima Patel had told her that it would restore the shine. Damien didn't think it had made any difference to Mammy's dry, wiry hair but the whey had smelled better than raw onion or molasses.

Finally, Da had relented. 'Take that puss off yer face now, Agnes,' he'd said impatiently, 'anyone would think it was lashin' outta the heavens!'

They'd retreated to the car, where they'd silently eaten their picnic of corned beef sandwiches, prawn flavoured crisps and shortbread, washed down with Mammy's brownish-coloured homemade lemonade (sweetened with molasses).

'Feckin' waste o'time,' Da had grumbled, crumpling his crisp packet, 'pure shite out.'

'Told you so, Albert,' Mammy had muttered with a smug smile on her face.

Damien still remembers the day he accompanied Da to Mr O'Keeffe's automobile workshop, crawling along the verge of the road in the VW which was making a strange noise.

'Engine's banjaxed,' he'd said to Mrs O'Keeffe, who had a messy desk in a corner of the workshop, 'sounds like beetles chirpin' inside it.'

'Engine's makin' a noise, Rory,' she'd shouted to Mr O'Keeffe, who was draining the sump of a Ford Zodiac.

'What kinda noise, Maura?'

'Crickets!' she'd shouted.

She had long, horsey teeth and no chin and reminded Damien of Princess Anne.

They'd left the VW with Mr O'Keeffe and had caught the Number 10 bus home. Sitting side-by-side, munching prawn-flavoured crisps, Da had remarked to Damien: 'She has some chompers on her, has Maura O'Keeffe. She'd have no bother knawin' an apple through a tennis racquet.'

After Da died, they'd asked Mr O'Keeffe to sell the VW. No one in the family could bear to get into it ever again.

Damien

The sun is starting to dip behind the horizon and the heat of the verandah is evaporating into the grey dusk. Long shadows are falling across the lawn and the black shapes of swallows returning to their nests are outlined against the apricot sky.

'Sundowner time,' says Damien, smiling wryly. 'Happy hour, ha-ha!'

He stretches out his long legs, before heaving himself out of the worn old chair and makes his way to the kitchen where he pours himself a double tot of whiskey. He puts a disc into the CD player and returns to the verandah where he eases his large frame into the chair. Strains of Beethoven's *Moonlight Sonata* fill the empty spaces and he leans back with his eyes closed.

Da used to love classical music, especially composers like Mozart, Chopin and Beethoven. He had an old portable tape recorder and would pop a cassette into it, turn up the volume and lean back in his armchair, puffing on his pipe. Damien had grown to love the sound of Beethoven's

34

piano concertos, especially *Fur Elise* and *Moonlight Sonata* and had longed to be able to play the piano himself. When Da was at work he'd listen to the cassettes, whilst lying on the floor, lost in his thoughts. He'd borrow library books about famous composers and read them late into the night. The next day he'd share what he'd read with Da.

'It was Beethoven's da who taught him to play music,' he'd said earnestly. 'He was an alcoholic and used to beat his son if he made mistakes and lock him in a cellar to make him practise. Wee Beethoven had to stand on a footstool to reach the keys and he'd be weepin' while his father flogged him.'

Da would listen intently, puffing on his pipe, while Mammy smiled and shook her head, winking at Maeve.

'What a horrible da,' Maeve said, screwing up her little face. 'He should've been locked in the cellar himself!'

'He started goin' deaf when he was only twenty-six and died of Cirrhosis and Syphilis when he was fifty-six. It was durin' a thunderstorm and . . . '

'Who's *Sir Osis* and *Sir Phyllis*?' Maeve had interrupted. Mammy had looked at Da and frowned, her cheeks flushing brick red.

'Cirrhosis is liver damage from drinkin' too much Guiness,' Da had replied.

'And *Sir Phyllis*?'

No one had answered.

35

For a long time after Da died, Damien had been unable to listen to music and, if by chance he ever heard the melodic, nostalgic chords of *Fur Elise* or *Moonlight Sonata,* he would weep disconsolately. It was only after he had fallen in love with Mary that he started listening to music again.

Mary

Mary had never been able to tell anyone what happened between her and Seamus, not even Daddy, because he was so sick. She didn't really know, herself, what had happened.

She'd been at Bridget O'Malley's birthday party with Maeve and they had had too much to drink. Maeve had hooked up with Fearghus and Seamus had been trying to kiss Mary while they were dancing. She didn't like Seamus Rafferty, was almost afraid of him, and he had a bad reputation; people said that he and Rosheen Murphy were drug users.

'Sure, you're a fine one, Mary O'Mara,' he'd drooled, his eyes looking drugged-out and dazed. His breath had smelt of stale cigarettes and Guiness and she'd turned her head away in disgust.

'Eff off, will ya, Seamus,' she'd slurred, as the room spun around her, 'sure, you're wasted.'

She remembers feeling dizzy and a bit nauseous and had decided to go home. She'd been trying to retrieve her coat from the cupboard under the stairs but there were so many coats on the floor. Seamus had followed her and had tried to kiss her again. She remembers trying to fight him off and waking up half an hour later, spreadeagled on the coats, with her legs apart and her knickers in disarray. When she'd staggered to the toilet, there was blood.

She'd been frozen in a state of silent shock and horror when she'd realised that Seamus had taken her virginity. She knew that she hadn't given it to him – he had taken it from her. She could never get it back, she could never be the same again and she had lost the one thing that she had been saving for Damien. Her thoughts were consumed with her shame, her regret and her loss, and everyone had thought she was so sad because of Daddy having cancer. And then, two months later, she had discovered that she was pregnant. She had wept and wept and cried out to God for help until, finally, she'd told Seamus and he'd agreed to marry her. Everyone had been shocked, especially Maeve, but Mary could tell no one. They'd never believe her anyway.

They'd had a simple little ceremony and Seamus had moved into Daddy's house, which had seemed to suit him very well. He had continued partying and using drugs while Mary nursed her father. Two months after the wedding she'd miscarried the baby and it was all over. She'd wept bitterly over the loss of her child but a part of her had felt relief that she was not giving birth to a baby who had been conceived unwittingly in a coat cupboard. Most of all, she'd wept over the loss of her future with the man she loved with all her heart.

She and Seamus had stayed together for two years, existing in the same house, while he shagged Rosheen (and God knows who else) and, when Daddy went into remission, they'd moved to the city while Mary finished her teaching degree. After she'd graduated she'd found a position teaching English at the Convent and they'd returned to Daddy and his declining health. Early, one cold wet morning, he lost his battle with cancer and died in his bed, while Mary kept a vigil at his bedside.

She'd sat alone, holding his thin cold hand with its raised purple veins, listening to the rain lashing against the window pane, and had never before felt so desolate and alone. She had longed to breathe her life into his, to resurrect him from death and feel a gentle warmth course through his skeletal body once more and she'd willed him back to life. But she knew then that the spirit of Frank O'Mara had departed forever to be reunited with Ma and that she was now officially an orphan.

Frank left the cottage to Mary in his will and she finally told Seamus to leave which he did without much fuss; he'd simply packed his bags and moved in with Rosheen. But, before he left he'd sneered at her and spat out the words that had stung her to the core. 'The best part o'you ran down yer ma's leg! Yer as useless as tits on a bull, Mary.'

She'd never felt such hatred and loathing as she had felt at that moment.

She knew that the church would denounce her and that God could never forgive her – and neither could Damien whom she'd heard was at seminary, studying to enter the priesthood. She knew too that she was a sinner, damaged goods, and had broken her marital vows. She'd long been chiselled by the church's most effective tool, guilt, and *mea culpa, mea culpa* was her mantra. Sister Evangelina had taught the girls that impurity was a very grave sin and that their bodies were the temple of the Holy Ghost. Mary had been impure and her body had carried the devil's spawn.

She'd poured her heart and soul into her teaching, returning home each evening to Rufus. She knew that people were gossiping about her after the divorce, whispering behind their hands, like they'd done when Maeve's da had committed suicide and she never went back to Mass for fear that she would be excommunicated. Anyway, how could God ever forgive her for conceiving a child in a coat cupboard? And what curse might have been on that child if it had lived? The fruit of the loins of that despicable scum bastard, Seamus Rafferty.

She never told Maeve the truth and they avoided mentioning Damien's name but, through it all, Maeve and Fearghus had never forsaken her and their loyalty to her had never wavered. She knew that Maeve needed to hear the truth but, somehow, Mary could never bring herself to speak of it and her filthy secret had been kept buried deep inside her.

Maeve

Maeve composes herself before she starts the e-mail. She doesn't want to sound desperate or begging and must choose her words carefully. Perhaps she should allude to the fact that she and Damien are not getting any younger, that the boys are now teenagers and will soon be spreading their wings . . . and, yes, she will mention that she misses her brother enormously. Should she mention Mary? Probably best if she doesn't. Let bygones be bygones.

They'd seen Mary the past weekend when she'd come for Sunday dinner. As always, she had looked lovely, almost ethereal, Maeve had thought. She was wearing a soft cotton frock which had clung to her slim frame and her hair was still as thick and black as it had been when they were young (although Maeve thought she'd spotted a few grey strands). Her skin was glowing and seemed almost translucent (although up close Maeve thought it was showing wee signs of ageing). Still, she'd had to admit that Mary was a beauty and had weathered well – far better, in fact, than Maeve herself. 'Will you look at the size o' you, Mary!' she'd exclaimed, running her eyes enviously over her friend's slender frame, 'how'd you manage to stay so trim?'

Mary had looked surprised, as though she'd never contemplated the size of her body in relation to anyone else's. 'Cyclin', I guess,' she'd shrugged, 'keepin' busy. I do eat, but I can't cook like you. Never took to it like you and your mammy.'

Maeve runs her fingers over the slight bulge around her midriff. She looks at her reflection in the silver frame she's holding. *I look just like Mammy,* she thinks, frowning. The same reddish-gold hair before it started to go grey, the pale blue-green eyes and the ruddy cheeks and freckles. 'Wholesome', that's what Mammy used to say, 'you may not be a beauty, darlin', but you're wholesome-lookin'.'

'Like a fat Irish cook,' mutters Maeve, smoothing her hair down and tucking it behind her ears.

She'd been happy watching her friend become so animated when she and young Damien had been bantering . . . *Ah, but they're both so sharp and quick-witted,* she thinks, *words flyin' back and forth like tennis balls bein' smashed over the net . . . such a shame she never had a child of her own. She would have been a great mammy. She's so unworldly and almost mesmerisin' with those huge blue eyes and dark eyelashes on her; how could she have chosen Seamus over Damien? Ah well, to be sure, life is full o' surprises . . .*

Maeve has never said it to anyone, not even to Mary, but sometimes she wonders if other people feel the way she does – waiting for something to happen, as though life had short-changed them and what they'd expected doesn't really exist. Did other people feel as though they were acting through life and were waiting to be found out and exposed? (Coming, ready or not . . .) and did they feel, like she did, that they could only be real when they were alone? Damien once told them that Yeats said that 'life is a long preparation for something that never happens'. Well, he understood.

She doesn't remember feeling like this when Damien was still here.

A dog walker strolls past with a Scottish terrier on a leash. Maeve watches the small black, short-legged dog with its beard and bushy eyebrows, lift its leg against the lamp post before continuing on its walk.

Sister Evangelina used to have a Scottie dog called Angus and she'd spend hours brushing and trimming his wiry coat and beard and eyebrows. Angus was moody and feisty and would growl at the girls if they came too close. Maeve had once tried to draw him during art class and Sister Evangelina had laughed and said that her drawing looked like an aardvark with a hat on it. Maeve had been upset but she didn't know what an aardvark was.

'What's an *art fart,* Dami?' she'd asked on their way home from school.

He'd laughed and ruffled her hair.

'It's an *aardvark,* Maeve, an ant eater. I'll show you when we get home.'

He'd taken her up to his bedroom and shown her a picture of one in an encyclopaedia and she'd been fascinated by its long snout, rabbit ears and kangaroo tail. She didn't think her drawing looked anything like that.

'It lives in Africa,' Damien had explained.

'Where's Africa?' Maeve had asked.

He'd shown her the continent of Africa on his rotating world globe which he kept on his bookcase and she'd spun the globe on its axis.

'Africa's a *looong* way from home,' she'd said.

'Aye, so it is, Maeve,' said Damien, 'a very long way from home.'

His bedroom was always neat and orderly. It had a single bed pressed up against the wall and there was an old telescope resting on the window ledge. Da had erected shelves on the opposite wall and, on the top shelf, Damien had displayed some of the model aircrafts he'd assembled over the years – a *Cessna*, a *Spitfire* and a *Messerschmitt*. Maeve and Mary used to watch, fascinated, as Damien glued bits of balsa wood together, before skimming them with tissue paper. He'd sit, frowning as he concentrated, his dark hair flopping over his forehead, his long fingers deftly glueing the pieces together, almost not breathing. The girls didn't dare move until he'd looked up, satisfied, and exhaled deeply.

On the next shelf was a row of matchbox cars, a soldier Action Man, a Rubik Cube, a Teenage Mutant Ninja Turtle and the antique tin box that Da had given him. The bottom shelves were sagging with books by Enid Blyton, Roald Dahl, Lewis Carroll, A A Milne and C S Lewis, alongside volumes of *Best Loved Bible Stories, The Hardy Boys, A Child's Garden of Verses* and *My Family and Other Animals.* Damien would never throw out a book. On his desk under the window was a rusty swing-arm lamp, a Peter Rabbit mug with a broken handle, full of pens and pencils, a framed photograph of Mammy and Da posing proudly beside the VW and a leather-bound Bible.

After they'd had dinner that evening Damien had helped Maeve to draw the Scottie dog again.

'That dog is the only creature Sister Evangelina loves,' Mammy had said dismissively, shaking the crumbs from the checkered table cloth. 'I thought nuns took a vow of charity?'

'They take a vow of *chastity*, Agnes,' Da had replied from behind his newspaper.

'What's chastity?' Maeve had asked.

Mammy's cheeks had flushed and she'd glanced at Da.

'It's bein' pure, my love,' Da had answered, poking at the tobacco in his pipe bowl with the sharp point of a blade on his Swiss army knife.

Maeve smiles at the memory. She takes the picture of Mammy and Da from the dresser and stares into their young optimistic faces, blinking into the sun with not even the vaguest notion of what the future held.

She sighs and begins her e-mail.

Damien

Damien tosses and turns in his narrow bed. He looks at the bedside clock: three o'clock. Suicide hour. The silence is oppressive; even the cicadas have stopped chirping. He lies awake, staring into the darkness, until a pale line of yellow appears through the gap in the curtains. In the distance he can hear the faint crowing of a rooster. *Didn't Peter deny Christ before the rooster crowed?*

He pulls on his jeans and heads for the bathroom before making his way to the little stone church. He quietly opens the heavy, wooden side door and is assailed by the smell of musty prayer books, incense and St Joseph's lilies. He proceeds to the altar and kneels on the worn burgundy carpet. Above him the light is just starting to shine through the stained glass windows, illuminating the gold crucifix on which the lifeless body of Christ is hanging.

The body of Christ . . . But He's not dead, He's risen, while I am just a mortal man, flesh and bone, a whited sepulchre. Did I think that I could escape the storms of life by bein' married to the church, by doin' good works to merit my salvation? What is the church anyway? It's not God. It's flawed, imperfect men and women, just like me. Sinners, all of us, saved by grace. I'm no different to Dorothy and Cynthia and all those other deluded sinners who have put me on a pedestal like the marble statues of their patron saints; who come to me seekin' absolution. All these years I've been relyin' on my own righteousness and religious works, tryin' to be good enough. And I'll never be good enough. What did the prophet Isaiah say? 'Your nakedness will be exposed and your disgrace will also be seen . . .' 7

'Oh, God, have mercy on my soul!' he cries, as he rises to his feet and hurries out of the church.

Dawn is breaking and the garden is bathed in pale, gentle sunshine. A chorus of birdsong signals the start of the day and the sound of generators and car engines heralds the beginning of the working week. Damien returns to the house, grabs the keys of his ancient Land Rover and Da's old Bible from the kitchen table and climbs behind the wheel. He places the Bible next to the rope on the passenger seat and reverses onto the dusty road, then accelerates out of the town, turning off the main road and heading towards the remote bushveld. The glaring sun is now almost blinding him and tears are starting to trickle down his cheeks. He wipes them away with the back of his hand and stares straight ahead at the thick bush and acacia trees and the granite hills and rocks that look hazy through the blur of his tears.

Finally he arrives at a secluded spot under a marula tree. The minutes tick by, as he sits in silence behind the wheel. What he is about to do is what Da had done thirty years ago. *Can I do*

47

this to Maeve? he thinks. *Can I cause her more of the pain that Da caused us, the pain that never goes away? Can I inflict the same shame on her that Mammy had to endure until the day she died?*

He clutches the Bible to his chest, as fresh tears course down his face. He remembers the words of a Psalm . . . *Answer me when I call to you, my righteous God. Give me relief from my distress; be merciful to me and hear my prayer.*

He sits crumpled over the steering wheel, his shoulders heaving, as he weeps. He weeps for the loss of the life he had thought he would have, for the loss of Da, for the loss of his freedom and the loss of the woman he'd thought he would marry.

Minutes pass as images flash before him: Mammy and Da, Maeve and Mary and the one ghastly, unforgettable image that he has never been able to erase of Da's grey lifeless body slumped over the steering wheel; the open, vacant, unseeing eyes, the clenched hands and the thin line of saliva trickling from his mouth. He sits for what seems like hours until he feels a gentle warmth rise slowly from his belly and begin to course through his body. He takes Da's Bible from the seat beside him and it falls open at the book of Ephesians: *For it is by grace you have been saved, through faith; and this is not from yourselves, it is the gift of God – not by works, so that no one can boast.*

Shards of sunlight are slashing through the branches of the marula tree, as an unexpected revelation begins to unfold. There is another way. He closes the Bible and places it on the seat beside him. A yellowing piece of paper flutters to the floor and he bends to retrieve it. Written in his distinctive flowing handwriting is the poem he's always loved, the poem he used to read to Mary and Maeve in front of the fire.

The Journey

One day you finally knew
what you had to do and began,
though the voices around you
kept shouting
their bad advice -
though the whole house
began to tremble
and you felt the old tug
at your ankles.
'Mend my life!'
each voice cried.
But you didn't stop.
You knew what you had to do,
though the wind pried
with its stiff fingers
at the very foundations,
though their melancholy
was terrible.
It was already late
enough, and a wild night
and the road full of fallen
branches and stones.

But little by little,
as you left their voices behind,
the stars began to burn
through the sheets of clouds,
and there was a new voice
which you slowly
recognised as your own,
that kept you company
as you strode deeper
and deeper
into the world,
determined to do
the only thing you could do -
determined to save
the only life that you could save. 8

He meditates on the familiar words. Does he have the courage to listen to his own voice and leave the smooth sailing of his comfort zone and risk setting sail into a new life? One that will require a death of some kind, a letting go of everything safe and familiar? Well, the best sailors aren't born in smooth waters. Da's voice comes back to him. 'Integrity. Tis the only thing that matters, son . . . if you have it, nothin' else matters.'

His clouded mind is now crystal clear. He knows what he must do. He folds the paper carefully and tucks it back into the Bible before turning the key in the ignition. The engine splutters into life and the acrid smell of diesel wafts through the rusty air vents.

Slowly, Father Damien makes his way home.

Mary

She takes the dry, paper-thin oak leaf gently between her thumb and forefinger and holds it up to the light. The intricate dark-red vein pattern is outlined against the deep russet gold of the leaf. Sister Evangelina said that oak leaves symbolise strength, endurance, faith and eternity and that the oak tree is the king of trees. She smiles, remembering the day she'd found the perfectly-shaped leaf after their swim in the stream and slides it gently between the pages of her book: *The Selected Poems of W B Yeats.* She reads the inscription on the fly leaf, the words she's read so many times before.

To my dearest Mary,

Had I the heaven's embroidered cloths,
Enwrought with golden and silver light,
The blue and the dim and the dark cloths
Of night and light and the half-light;
I would spread the cloths under your feet:
But I, being poor, have only my dreams;
I have spread my dreams under your feet;
Tread softly because you tread on my dreams 9

With all my love, Damien

She can still recall the feel of him, the warmth of his skin, the prickle of his stubble against her cheek, the musky smell of him and the taste of lipstick and salt and Guiness, as she breathed his hot breath that night under the porchlight. For years she's relived that moment over and over again in her mind. Months later she came across a new Mary Oliver poem:

> *I know someone who kisses the way*
> *A flower opens, but more rapidly . . . 10*

> *She knew,* she thought then, *she understood.*

Try as she may, she can never stop the memories from sliding back unannounced, without prior arrangement or warning, leaving her feeling sad and unsettled. Sometimes it will be the smell of a summer evening or the way the light falls at a particular moment, sometimes the notes of a song or the timbre of a voice like Damien's deep, lilting voice. After she'd married Seamus there had been a few occasions when she was convinced that she'd seen Damien and her heart had started racing but, on closer inspection, she'd discovered that it wasn't him and she'd felt an overwhelming melancholy.

She closes the book and puts it in her basket. This term her English class will be studying the poetry of Mary Oliver, starting with *The Journey,* one of Damien's favourite poems. It was Miss O'Leary who ignited his love for poetry and he had introduced Mary and Maeve to the poet's works. They used to mimic Miss O'Leary saying *poo-etry,* giggling every time they said the word. Damien said that the poet had born 'heavy burdens' (which Mary later discovered meant sexual abuse) but that she confronted the dark places in search of the light, exploring the wonder and pain of nature, learning to accept what cannot be changed. He said that Oliver's critics called her verse 'simplistic' and 'plain' but he thought that it taught people who didn't know how to love poetry, to love it.

Mary pictures him reciting *The Journey* to her and Maeve when they were lying under the oak tree or sitting in front of the fire, drinking hot cocoa and listening to the driving blizzard outside. Somehow, the sound of the howling bitter wind had made the poem come alive. His face had been illuminated by the flickering glow from the fire and his dark hair had flopped forward as he read. Later, they'd toasted marshmallows, turning them slowly until they puffed up and turned golden and Mary had felt like the happiest girl in the world.

'Ah, well, Rufie,' she sighs, 'it's better that we don't know what lies ahead. To be sure, we'd say we can't do it. We just have to keep goin', keep smilin' . . .' She strokes his arched back and he rubs his face against her. 'I'll be headin' to school now, my beauty. Catch you later.'

She throws her packed lunch into the basket, gives Rufus a final rub and closes the door of her little cottage. She's looking forward to the start of the new term, to new challenges and new faces in her English class and to having her days full again. Bridget O'Hara is taking maternity leave and, for the first time in its history, the Convent is allowing a male teacher to enter its hallowed walls. Niall O'Donovan will be filling in for Bridget and she's asked Mary to keep an eye out for him. Her bicycle is propped up against the wall and she breathes a sigh of relief that the sun is out. She prefers to cycle to school but often has to take the Number 10 bus, due to the inclement weather. It rumbles past the cottage every hour, causing the antique mahogany dresser in the sitting room and the tallboy in the bedroom to tremble, leaving the faint smell of burnt oil in its wake,.

She puts her basket over the handlebars and pedals off down the narrow road; past the hedgerows thick with fuschia and monbretia, over the little bridge, past Mr Patel's shop and finally through the imposing iron school gates. A red VW Polo pulls up next to her and a sandy-haired young man gets out.

'You must be Niall?' she says, shyly, dismounting and tucking the loose strands of hair behind her ears.

'I am, to be sure. How'ya doin'?'

She puts out her hand. 'Mary Rafferty. Your body guard.'

He smiles and his brown eyes crinkle at the corners. *Handsome,* thinks Mary. *The Convent will be explodin' with ragin' female hormones, schoolgirl crushes . . .* He relieves her of her basket and follows her down the cold, musty, flagstoned corridor. Pink-cheeked schoolgirls are gathered together in little huddles, their skirts the regulatory two inches below their knees, whispering behind their hands. *By next week your skirts will be two inches above your knees,* she thinks, smiling. Straight ahead of them, mounted on a high shelf in a corner of the passage, is a blue and white statue of The Blessed Mother, her hands outstretched in benediction over the sinners below.

'Mornin' Miss! Mornin' Sir!' the girls chorus, before exploding into giggles.

'Prepare yourself, Niall,' laughs Mary, 'a teenage girl is a force of nature.'

He smiles. 'I'll be needin' your advice, then, Mary, so I will.'

Cynthia

Father Damien fastens his dog collar in front of the chipped bathroom mirror, smoothes his hair back and makes his way across the dusty yard to his old Land Rover. It's still dark outside but dawn will be soon be breaking. He's in a hurry to get out into the bush to set up the Holy Communion table before the little group of parishioners arrives to celebrate Mass on this glorious Easter Sunday morning.

Cynthia has organised an Easter egg hunt amongst the rocks and boulders and has brought hot cross buns and filter coffee for the adults. Dorothy will be coming too, ferrying Patience Tshabalala and Beauty Moyo and some of the other parishioners and Jerry has offered to bring any other stragglers. She breathes in the fresh clean air and settles herself on a curved grey rock. It's always so lovely up in the hills in the early morning, before the baking sun starts to smother everything with its fierce rays and when no other humans are within sight. The granite boulders and overhanging balancing rocks have been weathered into strange shapes, like camels and mushrooms, and are streaked with flashes of orange, red and brown. Far across the hills she can see the big wooden cross erected by Father Odilo many years ago.

What must it be like to pastor a church so far away from your homeland? she wonders. *To leave behind the folk that you love and to give up everything to serve God in total obedience and surrender?*

Father Damien has always seemed different to the other clergy, more human to Cynthia, and she has to admit that she has wrestled with feelings that are inappropriate towards a man of the cloth. But she had felt drawn to him the minute she first met him ten years ago. She'd been surprised that such a fine-looking man had chosen to become a priest and deny his flesh, when surely there must have been numerous young women vying for his affections and he could have had a very different sort of life? She picks idly at a piece of yellow lichen growing on the rock. Well, who is she to question a vocation? A colourful blue-headed lizard emerges from a crevice and lifts its head curiously, scrutinising her intently for a few seconds, before scuttling away.

Cynthia feels ashamed when she frequently finds herself gazing at Father D in his vestments instead of concentrating on the Mass. She knows that she should be confessing her impure thoughts, but how can she confess them to the very one at whom they are directed? And she often has to reprimand herself when they are hiking with the walking group, as it is then that she is inclined to forget that Father D is a priest, married to the church. She sighs. It's just that he's so attractive in his T-shirt and shorts, with his strong muscular legs and golden skin. She likes to walk behind him when they're hiking and watch his calf muscles contract with each step he

56

takes. She'll never forget the day they took a dip in the rock pool and she'd seen his bare chest with just the right amount of glistening body hair. (Unlike Jerry, whose body hair was like a pelt and his back like a kudu skin.) She's sure that Father D had cast an admiring glance over her own body in her bathing suit but perhaps she was just imagining it.

It's not just his physical appearance that is so attractive to Cynthia; it's his honesty and integrity, his kindness and compassion and his appreciation of poetry and the arts. That's what she'd loved about her darling Michael, who had died after that terrible road accident when their Emma was only four years old. She'd stayed by his side night and day at the hospital, listening to the hissing of the tubes and pipes attached to his poor ravaged body, watching the heart monitor anxiously, until they'd said he was on the road to recovery. She'd gone home to take a shower, when she'd received the call. Michael was dead. She'd held the phone to her ear, as her body had slithered down to the floor and she'd lain in a crumpled heap, wailing, 'not that! Oh, please God, not that!' She'd kept his ashes in an earthenware vase, unable to part with them, until Father D had gently persuaded her to inter them in the garden of rememberance. He'd dug the hole himself and the two of them had commended Michael's remains to the earth. Dust to dust, ashes to ashes. After that, Cynthia had begun to heal.

She sighs, stretching her shapely legs and dusting herself down. She really shouldn't be thinking these thoughts, especially on Easter Sunday. Sunrise flashes fire in shades of orange and purple and pink over the sculptured rocks and balancing boulders and nature begins to stir. The dry grass rustles as lizards emerge to seek a patch of sun and bird calls echo across the granite hills. A majestic black eagle soars in the sky above, searching for a rock hyrax as its prey. She turns, shielding her eyes from the sun which is gently kissing the horizon. Father D's rusty old Land Rover pulls up, followd by several cars, leaving clouds of red dust in their wake, and bleary-eyed passengers emerge. She takes her basket of shiny, colourful Easter eggs and disappears to hide them among the rocks, while Jerry quickly retrieves his binoculars from around his neck and follows the trajectory of the magnificent bird. 'Hell, what a sight!' he exclaims, 'the black eagle. *Aquilla verreauxii.* Bloody marvellous!'

Dorothy is wearing big brown brogues and brown slacks which cling to her broad bottom. She treads gingerly over the mounds of dung and rock hyrax droppings before settling into a camp chair. Its canvas seat stretches in protest. 'Did you know that the soaring eagle represents the resurrection of Christ?' she asks excitedly, 'how awesome is that on Easter Sunday?'

Jerry produces his worn old bird book and turns to the section on eagles. 'The black eagle is coal black,' he reads, 'with a white V on its shoulders. Hell, what a magnificent creature! Bloody marvellous!'

The service begins with a few well-known hymns, led by Jerry on his guitar. Slowly, the singing gets louder and louder, with the pure African voices harmonising together, until the hills reverberate with praise and the sun in all its glory shines across the hillside. Father Damien, in his white vestments, stands on a hilly little outcrop of rocks and looks out at his motley crew of disparate, multi-coloured parishioners, singing heartily. He feels a deep sadness in his soul that this will be his last Easter Sunday Mass.

Cynthia scolds herself for her loss of concentration at the sight of Father D in his white robes with his arms outstretched, his large body outlined against the golden sky, like the statue of Christ the Redeemer in Rio de Janeiro.

Niall

For the past few weeks Mary has been looking forward to arriving at school every morning, hoping that Niall will be there early too. Her heart flutters with anticipation and she blushes as he pulls in, just as she is dismounting her bicycle. 'Fancy that!' he says, smiling, 'perfect timin'.' She doesn't know that he deliberately plans his arrival to coincide with hers. They've established a routine of sharing a pot of tea in the staff room before the clanging of the bell announces the start of lessons. Niall regales her with amusing stories about his experiences teaching history to bored pubescent girls and she listens intently, laughing at his impersonations and mimicry. 'We were discussin' *The Troubles* last week and Molly Finnigan said, Sir, don't you think we need to go deeper? The whole class broke out in snorts and giggles and Sinead Ryan was flutterin' her eyelashes at me. She'd written *I love you* on her eyelids with a black Magic Marker!'

Mary blushes and shakes her head. 'That Sinead suffers from a double dose of original sin, Niall. She should be sent to Sister Ethel Mary – she'll sort her out soon enough. Don't know how you manage to keep control.'

She swallows the last dregs of her tea as Sister Madeleine starts swinging the heavy old cast iron bell. Its clanging sound reverberates down the corridors and into the classrooms. The nun's round, puffy face is turning pink from the exertion and her protruding teeth bite into her bottom lip as she sways from side to side, clutching the bell in both her hands. Her wooden cross necklace swings rhythmically in time with the bell and her large round buttocks wobble, while the tassle on the corded belt around her waist sways in the opposite direction. Mary grimaces, remembering having to recite the rosary under the watchful eye of Sister Madeleine, kneeling in a row on the hard wooden floor of the chapel with the other fourteen-year old girls, trying not to focus on the hairs sprouting out of her chin. 'Remember the twenty Mysteries, girls . . . one *Our Father*, three *Hail Marys* and one *Glory Be.*'

She gathers her books and bag and Niall gets to his feet, wiping his mouth hurriedly with the back of his hand. 'Experience, Mary,' he says, 'years of experience. But I have to admit that teachin' girls is a different experience altogether.' He hesitates. 'Been wantin' to ask you . . . the fair's come to town . . . passed the fairground on my way home yesterday. Would you care to accompany me there Saturday?'

Mary's face flushes with pleasure. It's been years since she went to a fair. Daddy once took her and Maeve to the circus at the fairground when they were six and she's never forgotten the thrill and excitement of the big tent, the sound of the roaring crowds and the barrel organ; the acrobats, trapeze artists and jugglers and the sight of the huge grey elephants waving their trunks as they pooped. She'd never seen such enormous poops before. She'd cowed with fear when the lions roared with their heads thrown back, baring their sharp yellow teeth against the red of their gums and she'd cried when their handler cracked his whip. But, out of all the circus acts, it was the clowns that had terrified her the most.

'That would be just grand, Niall,' she says, smiling.

He watches her hurry away, the loose strands of her hair fluttering against her face. She's wearing a duck-egg blue blouse with tiny white raised spots on the fabric. Niall had found himself wanting to touch the fabric and run his fingers over the dots and over her creamy skin. But there's something strange about her, something he can't put his finger on; a sadness inside perhaps, as though she's hiding a secret. He's finding himself being drawn to her more and more and is sometimes mesmerised by her ethereal beauty. Those dimples that appear when she presses her lips together and those big blue eyes, like deep pools of water that could drown a man when he's not looking.

He gathers his thoughts as he hurries out of the staffroom. *Don't be an eejit now, man. You've had yer heart broken before. Take it slowly*

Damien

His letter to the Holy See, requesting an *indult of exclaurstration* for a year had not been as difficult to write as the following one, requesting permanent dispensation from his priestly vows and obligations. He had spent hours composing the letter, as he tried to explain that he had lost his vocation and felt that he could no longer live the life of a priest with integrity. He'd also had endless online counselling sessions with the Bishop, who had tried to convince him that he was 'destined for great things' and would find 'ordinary life' boring.

'You'll come crawling back, Damien,' he'd pronounced, after exhausting every avenue of persuasion. 'You'll miss the priestly life; there's no greater honour than to be God's representative here on earth.'

But ordinary life is all I want, Damien had thought. *Just to be a man.*

'You need to take a break, son, go back to Ireland, rediscover your calling. Once you've made the decision to leave the church, it won't be easy to come back.'

'I have made the decision, Bishop. My mind is clear about that. I won't be coming back.'

'If you leave, there will be no place for you in the system, Damien. Think about that.'

If it's a system, I don't want to be in it, Damien had thought.

Finally, after many months of anxiety and soul-searching, he had received a document from Rome granting a dispensation from the obligations of priestly ordination, including celibacy, and from religious vows. 'You are instructed to notify your congregation by announcing that you will be taking a sabbatical. When you have been replaced, I shall notify the parish officially,' the Bishop had ordered.

Telling Dorothy and Cynthia that he would be taking a sabbatical had been harder than he'd expected. Cynthia's eyes had welled up with tears and she'd wrung her hands, murmuring, 'what are we going to do? What am I going to do?' He'd been touched by her reaction and had wanted to hug her. 'Cynthia, lass,' he'd replied, touching her shoulder gently, 'you'll carry on just as you always have done; the walking group will continue . . . '

'But you don't understand,' she'd whispered, turning away.

Ah, but I do, he'd thought, *I do.*

Dorothy's face had flushed a deep brick red and she'd burst into tears, with snot pouring out of her nose. She'd removed her spectacles and wiped her face with the back of her hand, smearing mucous across her face. 'You're a traitor, Father D!' she'd cried, 'abandoning your flock, leaving us here in this dry bloody desert, while you go back to the green Emerald Isle . . . '

The shepherd who leaves his sheep is a hireling, Damien had thought.

'I've always dreamed of going to Ireland,' Dorothy had sobbed, 'why does God always destroy my dreams?' She'd taken huge gulps of air, almost hyperventilating, and had lumbered to the organ and thrown herself at it, pressing her fingers into the keys, pounding the pedals with her big heavy shoes, as the music reached a crescendo. Afterwards, spent and exhausted, she'd apologised to Damien for her outburst and had asked if she could take him to the airport when he departed.

'Dorothy, lass,' he'd said, softly, 'don't blame God for everything bad in your life. We're all given choices but with those choices come consequences. Think on that. But never doubt how much God loves you.'

How will she ever forgive me when she hears that I won't be returnin'? he'd thought.

He'd had a quiet word with Malcolm after Mass and suggested that Dorothy might need some support. 'And why don't you think about joining the walking group, Malcolm? You'd make some new friends and the exercise would help you to cope with yer grief.'

Malcolm had looked across at Dorothy and frowned; then he'd muttered something inaudible, before heading towards the table.

Mary

The months have flown by and Mary is enjoying the unfamiliar heady feeling of infatuation and the seemingly endless possibilities that lie ahead; the thrill of going out for dinner or just to the pub with Niall and having deep, intense conversations late into the night, laughing uproariously at his silly jokes. She'd never imagined she'd feel like this, never expected her life to fall into such a different rhythm. Of course, Niall is younger than she is and she can't imagine why he would want to spend time with her when there are so many pretty young lasses itching for his attention, but she's not going to dwell on that now and spoil the moment.

This morning she's woken with a feeling of excitement – the weather is fine and she has a date with Niall. She allows herself to dream while she lies back in her bubble bath, flicking the warm water over her thighs and breasts. She watches the frothy bubbles settle and then dissolve and evaporate, leaving a silky sheen on her skin. She turns the hot tap with her foot, causing her stomach muscles to contract and her rose-pink nipples to peep through the soapy water. Rufus watches her intently with his enigmatic green eyes.

'C'mere Rufie. I know you're hungry. You're always hungry but you'll just have to wait.' She stares at his perfect face with the smooth white *M* on his forehead and the little black freckles around his mouth and nose and reaches down to stroke him. 'Look at you there! Such a handsome boy.' He rolls onto his back and purrs contentedly.

She discards several outfits before she settles on a pair of jeans and a red sweater which clings softly to the shape of her body. She brushes her hair vigorously in front of the mirror and, for a brief moment, an image of a young Damien brushing her hair and cupping his hand around her curls with an elastic band between his teeth, flashes before her. The ghost of that unquestioning, innocent little girl, oblivious to what horror lay ahead, stares back at her. She'd been propelled unwittingly into another life, another world over which she had no control. *I wish I could start again*, she thinks, wistfully. *I wish I could re-write the story. It wouldn't be a fairy tale or a romance novel like those silly Barbara Cartland books that Maeve used to read. But it would have a happy ending.* She blinks back to reality and clucks. 'Ah, Mary. You're away with the fairies now!'

She decides to leave her hair loose, applies some red lipstick and slips her feet into her red pumps. She sprays some perfume behind her ears and takes a final look in the mirror, just as the doorbell rings. Grabbing her bag, she skips down the stairs, singing, 'Heigh, ho, come to the fair!'

Niall

The atmosphere at the fairground is charged with an electric excitement. The barrel organ is thundering in the background, the ferris wheel is turning, lights are flashing and the horses on the carousel are bobbing up and down. 'D'ya remember that Joni Mitchell song?' asks Niall, bursting into song . . . 'and the seasons they go round and round, and the painted ponies go up and down, we're captured on the carousel of time . . . ' Mary nods and smiles, as she joins in, 'we can't return, we can only look behind somewhere we came, and go round and round and round in the circle game . . '[1] Her voice trails off and she blushes as Niall gazes at her lovingly.

The air is thick with the sugary smell of warm doughnuts, frying onions and diesel fumes. Niall pushes his way through the colourful crowd jostling towards the candy stall and buys Mary some sickly-sweet candyfloss. They try their luck at the tombola stall and she shrieks with laughter when she wins a box of chocolates. They wander around the fairground, admiring the prize cows and the pink, blue-ribboned pig, licking sno-cones while they soak up the warm rays of the sun. Every few minutes they pass a group of school girls dressed in tiny shorts and tight T-shirts, exposing their bare mid-riffs. As

Mary and Niall approach them they turn to each other and whisper and giggle behind their hands. *The gossip mill will be in overdrive on Monday*, thinks Mary, but she doesn't care. Right now, she feels like a child at the circus again. They ride the dodgem cars and the ferris wheel and her cheeks flush with excitement as she throws her head back and laughs, her hair billowing behind her.

'Will you join me for a pint o' Gat, Mary?' asks Niall as they make their way to the car park. She hesitates.

'Ah, go way outta that; of course you will,' he says, putting an arm around her shoulders and giving her a squeeze.

She smiles. 'That would be grand, Niall.'

The pub is warm and cosy, brimming with locals and a few unfamiliar faces. Niall finds a spot in a corner booth in front of the Victorian fireplace and, while he buys their drinks, Mary examines the black and white photographs on the tobacco-stained walls: *The Rolling Stones arrive at Dublin Airport (1965), Mohammad Ali vs Al 'Blue' Lewis (1972), A Farewell Kiss at Dublin Airport (1952), Princess Grace at the 1965 Irish Open Tennis Championships* . . .

Princess Grace . . . She and Maeve had watched a documentary about her life on

Daddy's old Box TV – her fairytale wedding to Prince Rainier, so handsome in his uniform, and then shattered and bowed with grief at her funeral; Caroline, veiled in black, Stephanie in a neck brace and Prince Albert holding his father's arm. Mary had thought Princess Grace was the most beautiful woman she had ever seen and had decided that one day she would have a daughter named Grace. Maeve had sighed and clasped her hands to her bosom at the reassuring sight of the handsome prince and his beautiful movie star bride in her pearl-studded wedding dress with its long train trailing behind her and had wept at the sight of the serene princess, lying in state in a dark wood coffin. Perhaps fairy tales don't come true, after all?

Mary looks around the busy pub. Sitting opposite her is a greying man in a green sweater and wool trousers speaking sign language to a much younger man. His arms are flailing and his fingers are jabbing the air and Mary wonders what he's saying. She studies him carefully, smiling at his sometimes graceful, sometimes comic and frantic movements. Mick O'Farrell, proprietor of *O'Farrell's Fine Meats* arrives and tips his cap. He heads for his usual spot behind the bar and shouts across to the signer in his high-pitched voice, 'what's the story, Rory?' The signer turns around and shouts back, 'ah, ya stingy bastard, O'Farrell! What's the craic?' Mary smiles and looks away.

Niall returns with two half-pints of Guiness and a fiddler strikes up a tune. Her feet start tapping to the music and she finds herself wanting to dance. Niall looks at her admiringly and lifts his glass in a toast. 'Bless yer little Irish heart – and every other Irish part!' He takes a long sip of beer and smiles, taking her hand.

'I had the best time today, Niall,' she says, flushing, 'haven't had such fun in donkeys' years.'

'Me too,' says Niall, kissing the back of her hand. 'I'm becomin' very fond o' you, Mary.'

They make their way across the busy car park and Niall opens the car door for Mary who slides in. They drive in silence until they pull up at the cottage and she turns to him. 'Will you be comin' in for a glass of wine then, Niall?'

'Yeah, sure I would,' he replies, beaming, his cheeks rosy from the Guiness and the warmth of the pub.

She opens the front door and Rufus greets them with a loud miaow, rubbing himself against their legs. The intoxicating scent of lilies permeates the cottage with their pungent sweetness and Niall looks admiringly around the cosy sitting room with its cream and green hues, floral-patterned cushions and vases of the white, trumpet-shaped flowers. He examines the silver-

71

framed photographs on the rosewood dresser and takes one in his hands.

'And who would these be, then?' he asks, staring intently at the picture.

Mary pauses. 'That's my best friend, Maeve, and her brother, Damien. We'd just won a game of doubles. I was fifteen then.'

'And a looker even then, Mary. Young Damien's a good-lookin' lad too.'

'He's a priest now,' says Mary softly, 'in Africa.'

'Yer coddin' me? A priest? What a waste of such a fine-lookin' lad!'

'Not to the church, he's not,' says Mary, her hand trembling as she pours the wine.

They settle onto the sofa with Rufus purring between them. Niall reaches across the cat and cups her face in his hand. He leans over to kiss her and as his lips touch hers, she turns her face away and his kiss lands on her cheek. He frowns and Mary can see the look of irritation on his face. Why would she suddenly reject his kiss when she's been giving him signals all day? He empties his wine glass and gets abruptly to his feet.

'Well, I'll be crackin' on then.'

She lets him out without saying a word. Niall looks at her uncomprehendingly and frowns again before he turns and walks away. She watches him striding towards his car, his hands in his pockets and his head down, then she closes the door and climbs the stairs wearily, clutching Rufus.

Mary

She lies still, staring into the darkness. Her mind is racing with tortured thoughts and questions.

Why did she spoil the end of a lovely day? What is she so afraid of? Will she ever be able to erase those hellish memories of Seamus? Will she ever be able to be intimate with a man again and not see that angry red face leering over her? And will she be forever haunted by the ghost of Damien and the faded dream of a different life with the only man she has ever loved?

Images of Seamus' pock-marked face flash before her, as she reflects on how the abuse had first started. At the beginning he would rage about small things, like a sticking drawer or a faulty light bulb or a lack of seasoning in the stew. Then he'd be irritated with her if she'd come home late from school and his dinner wasn't ready. He'd swear at the television if he didn't like the programme she was watching and had once thrown the remote control across the room and shattered Ma's Ming vase, which Daddy had discovered at a junk shop. The verbal abuse had progressed to physical violence and one night he'd kicked her in bed when she had rejected his advances; his bony foot had connected with her hip and she'd cried out in pain. He'd pulled her hair until chunks of it came out in his hand and his face had turned puce as he slapped her hard across her face, pinning her down on the bed, exhaling clouds of foul-smelling breath. 'Yer feckin' scum bastard fella's not here to defend ya now, Mary,' he'd sneered, 'yer a frigid bitch, that's what you are!'

74

She'd had to buy maximum cover make-up to hide the purple lesions and had lied to Maeve when she'd asked if that was a bruise she could see under Mary's eye. Just before she'd miscarried the baby, Seamus had kicked her in the stomach in a drunken rage, before slamming the door and leaving her on the floor. Thank God Daddy had been at the dairy. She'd crawled to the staircase and dragged herself up the stairs to the bedroom, before collapsing onto the bed. The pain had been excruciating. And then the blood had come – warm and red and sticky, pouring down her legs and she knew then that, finally, it was all over.

Shortly afterwards she'd had a disturbing dream. She had been nursing her baby girl named Grace and had been enraptured by her beauty and her sweet, subtle, powdery baby smell, her soft white flesh and tiny, perfect fingers wrapped around Mary's thumb. She'd been so caught up in that feeling of utter bliss and contentment that she'd wanted to capture the moment forever and be frozen in time. But, suddenly, Seamus had appeared at the door, demanding dinner and a hot bath. She'd hastily put her baby into the silver heart-shaped locket she was wearing around her neck and reluctantly obeyed her husband. As she bent over the bath, with the hot tap running and steam filling the bathroom, her locket had swung open and her baby had escaped. Only it wasn't her baby that had flown out of the locket – it was a terrible black stick insect, like a giant praying mantis. She'd watched helplessly, clutching the open, empty locket, as the insect flew up and away towards the ceiling, far above the steam, and disappeared.

She'd cried and wailed and sobbed for days after that, her mouth wide open in a tormented cry, like the twisted, foetal-faced creature in Edvard Munch's painting, *The Scream*. It had felt as though her pain and heartache were being caught up into a whirlpool of emotions, swirling around her, almost vibrating, like the twirling tongues of blood and fire in the background of the painting and she was being sucked into them. She'd thought then that she might die of grief, like the biblical Rachel, 'weeping for her children and refusing to be comforted, because they are no more'.12 She'd read somewhere that the female mantis bites off the head of the male after mating.

It was then that Daddy had been diagnosed with cancer and all Mary's energy had been diverted into trying to save him. She'd taken him to his chemotherapy sessions, held his head over the toilet bowl when he'd retched and vomited, wiped his brow with a cool cloth and administered his pain killers. She had kept a vigil at his bedside night after night, watching him slowly fade away and, when his breathing had become shallow and each breath had been

76

further apart, she'd put her head on his rattling chest and her arms around his thin wasted body and had listened to his heart pulse its final faint beat.

Afterwards she'd sat on the rocking chair beside his bed with her arms wrapped around her own body, sobbing for hours, while the rain lashed against the window pane and the branches of the chestnut tree swayed and groaned against the bitter wind. She hadn't cried like that again, not even at Daddy's funeral, where she had longed so desperately for Damien's calming presence. Maeve and Fearghus had carried her through those dark days afterwards; she could always depend on Maeve and Fearghus.

Her crying in the years after that had been a soundless shedding of tears, a releasing of overpowering emotions, a weeping which would begin as a trickle and become an unceasing stream, before becoming a trickle again and, finally, a sob.

You need help, Mary, she thinks. *You thought you'd put it all behind you. How did Paul in Sons and Lovers put it? You'll find you're always tumbling over the things you've put behind you.*[13]

As she drifts off to sleep, she reluctantly resolves that she will make an appointment with a therapist to try and put the past to rest.

Damien

Damien pulls his best shirt over his head, runs
his fingers through his hair and looks at his

reflection in the bathroom mirror. A section of his hair is standing up in a cowlick. 'Father Trendy,' he mutters, trying to flatten the loose strands. He could do with some of Da's *Brylcreem* right now.

It's Christmas Eve, the night of Cynthia's annual party, when all the local townsfolk and 'the strays' will be gathering at her home. Is he dressed correctly? He never knows how to dress for an occasion, for those times when he's in 'civvies' and not Father Damien in his 'frock' as Maeve had called it. Tonight he's wearing his only pair of jeans and a blue and white striped shirt, a birthday gift from Dorothy. Ah, well, she'll be pleased to see him in it, anyway. He's never been able to afford new clothes on his small stipend and it seems frivolous and selfish to him, when the bulk of his congregation live from hand to mouth. His vows of poverty, celibacy and obedience have never really troubled him, since he chose to sublimate his fleshly desires and made the choice to give up marriage and children in order to live a life serving God with an undivided heart. His desire had never been to be revered or esteemed by others or to appear strong and wise in the midst of others' weaknesses and he abhorred the idea of living his life in a fishbowl. What had his desire been, then?

His decision to leave the priesthood had been the hardest decision he had ever had to make but he knows, deep in his heart, that to maintain his integrity, it is the only solution. He knows too that, in leaving, he will lose his home, his job and his friends in order to be free, just to be human. His priestly training in morality had involved so many dos and don'ts – mostly don'ts – which had been easy enough to obey but now he finds himself wondering how they will apply to him once he steps deeper into the new life that awaits him.

He runs his fingers through his damp hair again. 'You need a good haircut, Father,' he murmurs, 'yer looking more and more like Father Trendy.' He smiles at the image of the comic creation, with his Elvis hairstyle and leather jacket and his puppet called Zak. *Why are people so surprised when they discover that priests are just ordinary men?* he ponders, *perhaps they're disappointed that their idols have feet of clay?*

When Damien was a schoolboy he used to wonder what Father Farwell's life was like in-between being a priest, or if there was even an in-between? Did he ever get lonely? Did he sometimes wish for a companion? What did he do for fun?

Maeve and Mary used to wonder about the nuns. 'What do they wear underneath their habits?' they would ask Mammy. 'Do they have hair, or is it all shaved off? Are they allowed to eat chocolate?'

'Ah, sure they eat chocolate!' Mammy had replied, dismissively, 'look at the size of Sister

Evangelina, for God's sake!'

Brother Enda had tried to be trendy for a while and had grown his hair into a mullet. He would strum an old tuneless guitar and sing *Morning has Broken* and *Let it Be*, as he hovered over the youngsters in his black cassock, looking like a vulture. Damien can still picture the rows of spotty kids, smiling tightly, cringing with embarrassment, as spittle flew from Brother Enda's mouth and the veins in his neck bulged. Seamus and his gang used to imitate Brother Enda and Damien had longed to be able to tell him to stop trying to be cool, to just be himself, but it would have seemed impertinent coming from a young lad.

God forbid that I should ever appear to be trying to be trendy, he thinks, smoothing his hair flat against his head.

He grabs the keys of the Land Rover and slams the back door behind him.

Maeve

Maeve kicks the door closed behind her, dumps

the bags of groceries on the kitchen table and removes her coat. Rain is lashing down outside and she's drenched. Fearghus is sitting in front of the fire, reading *The Irish Times*.

'Look at the state o' you, lass,' he mutters, without leaving his chair.

'It's lashin' out o' the heavens, Fearghus!' says Maeve, smoothing down her wet hair, 'I nearly took a hopper in Patrick Street.'

Fearghus is engrossed in his newspaper.

Maeve sighs. 'I'll go wet the tea.'

She boils the kettle while she unpacks the groceries. She must start preparing for Christmas dinner tomorrow, make the mince pies, set the table; there won't be much time in the morning.

'D'you suppose Mary will be bringin' her fella for Christmas dinner, Fearghus, love? It's been grand to see her happy and laughin' again.'

'Aye,' says Fearghus, turning the page, 'deserves a bit of happiness, so she does.'

Maeve pauses, as her thoughts turn to her brother in Africa. What sort of Christmas will he be having out there? Probably going to parties and dinners with all those lasses who fancy him, who secretly wish that he wasn't married to the church.

How she misses her beloved brother and the Christmases they used to have when Mammy and Frank were still alive. They didn't have much between them but Frank had always contributed towards the cost of the turkey and had brought whiskey for Mammy and fresh cream from the dairy to pour over the mince pies. They'd used the leftover cream to make 'Christmas gravy' and hot chocolate to drink after the meal (while Mammy and Frank drank the whiskey) and they'd roast chestnuts and marshmallows on the fire. Mammy's cheeks would glow and she'd laugh at Frank's jokes and the world had seemed so bright and happy then. The house used to smell of cinnamon and cloves and they'd lie in front of the fire after Christmas dinner with their bellies bursting, reciting *poo-etry*, giggling as they mimicked Miss O'Leary's accent:

> *'Twas da night before Christmas, when all troo da house,*

> *Not a creature was stirrin' not even a mouse.*
> 14

'Ah, Fearghus,' sighs Maeve, 'I wish Dami hadn't left us and gone so far away. Sure, I miss him – especially at Christmas.'

Feraghus grunts from behind his newspaper.

She carefully unwraps the cinnamon candle, ready to be placed in the bay window on Christmas Eve, just like Mammy used to do.

'Why do we put candles in the window at Christmas?' she'd asked Mammy when she was seven.

'To light the way for Mary and Joseph on their way to find the stable in Bethlehem,' she'd replied, assuredly.

'Och, Agnes!' Da had snorted, 'no wonder they were lost – they'd be on the wrong feckin' continent! Jesus would have been twenty years old by the time they got to Bethlehem on a donkey!' He'd turned to Maeve. 'It's actually a custom datin' from the seventeenth century, darlin', when the Penal Laws suppressed Catholicism and priests hid in fear of their lives; the candle was a signal that this was a Catholic home and any passin' priest was welcome to join the family to say the Mass.'

Mammy's cheeks had flushed and she'd muttered something under her breath.

Maeve takes the tea to Fearghus and settles into the armchair, tucking one leg under the other. She takes out her notepad and starts to write a list:

Whiskey

Turkey

Ham

Brussels sprouts

Crackers

Jelly

Custard

Cream

Fruit & nut cake mix

Quality Street

She pauses, as she takes a sip of tea. 'Will we be goin' to the Panto on Boxin' Day, Fearghus, love? Perhaps Mary will come with her fella?'

'Aye,' says Fearghus, not looking up from his newspaper.

Damien

Cynthia's home is festooned with twinkling fairy lights. Two car guards are ushering the various Land Cruisers and imported cars into parking bays along the driveway, as Damien pulls up in his old Land Rover and Dorothy arrives in her

Honda.

'Father D!' she cries, her face flushing, 'how lovely to see you, looking so handsome in my shirt!'

'Aye, it's grand, Dorothy,' he smiles, patting his chest awkwardly, 'you're a thoughtful lass, to be sure.'

They follow the other guests down a path into a wonderland of lights and Christmas decorations, with the strains of *Jingle Bell Rock* thumping in the background . . . *snowin' and blowin' up bushels of fun, now the jingle hop has begun!* Long tables, adorned with holly, streamers and crackers are set around the swimming pool and the bar counter is lined with colourful beverages of every type, with champagne bottles protruding from ice buckets.

Cynthia is herding the excited children together. 'See who'll be the first one to hear Santa's bell! He'll be coming over the roof with his reindeer!'

She looks up and sees Damien and her face breaks into her lovely smile which seems to come from deep inside her, opening like a flower and lighting her eyes. 'Welcome, Father D,' she says, ushering him to the head of the longest table. She's wearing white slacks with a blue-patterned scarf that matches her shirt, and her golden hair is curling around her animated face like a halo.

Damien watches the children playing, weaving in and out of the tables in their

Christmas hats, their hands full of sweets, while snacks are served and drinks refilled. The humid day has melted into a humid night and the air is smothering him like a wet blanket. In the distance he can hear the clicking sound of cicadas and the faint low crackle of thunder. He's grown to love the brief, sharp African thunderstorms which always bring such welcome relief from the searing heat; the dark and heady smell of moisture filling the air before the pattering of tiny raindrops, followed by the loud heavy plops of rain. He takes a mouthful of Cynthia's imported red wine and looks around him.

Seated to his right is Dorothy and to his left, Cynthia: his faithful handmaids, like Mary and Martha. Dorothy's cheeks are fiery red and her upper lip is glistening with perspiration. Next to her is Patience Tshabalala with her daughter, Pretty, sitting on her lap. Pretty is wearing a pink net ballet skirt with shiny white tights and ballet pumps. On her head is a jewel-encrusted crown and in one hand she's brandishing a wand. She studies Damien intently with her big brown, unblinking eyes, while she licks a green lolly pop she's holding in her other hand. Patience bends her head and whispers something in Pretty's ear. A flicker of light from a candle flutters across her cheekbones, illuminating her smooth ebony skin. Opposite Damien are Jerry and old Frank from the Salvation Army hostel. He has one long tooth protruding from his bottom lip, like a rhino horn, and a black eye patch over his left eye. He's wearing a tie with his weathered MOTH jacket and has his walking stick propped up against the chair beside him. Next to him is Gwen who has recently completed a spell at the Nervous Disorders hospital. She has always been a particularly demanding parishioner and Damien tries to avoid making eye contact with her. He greets old Frank across the table, cautiously moving the candle out of Pretty's reach.

'How are ya, Frank? Yer looking smart tonight.'

'Not getting any younger, Father,' he sighs, 'the *arthuritis* is playing up. Old age is not for sissies.'

Damien smiles and nods as his thoughts turn to another Frank. Memories come flooding back of Frank O'Mara accompanying Mammy to the Bingo before he got cancer. That was when she'd started smiling again and spraying *Anais Anais* behind her ears and on her wrists. Frank used to join them for icy cold Christmases when Mammy would cook a turkey with roast potatoes and Brussels sprouts. She'd teach them how to make 'Christmas gravy' from the liquid left in the pan and Maeve and Mary would make mince pies under her watchful eye, popping off-cuts into their mouths when Mammy wasn't looking. 'Don'tcha be makin' a right bags of it, now!' she'd scold them, swatting them with a dishcloth, 'I'll smack the arses off you both, so I will!' They'd shriek with laughter and run and hide behind Damien.

How he misses Maeve and her two boys and the warmth of being part of a family. He feels the familiar sharp stab of pain as he wonders how Mary is spending her Christmas Eve. Where is she now? He pictures her in a cosy cottage with children of her own, helping her prepare the meal, her black hair tumbling down her neck . . .

He's jerked back to the present by the ringing of a bell in the distance and the delighted squealing of the children. 'It's Santa! It's Santa!' they cry, as they turn their gazes to the black night sky. Little Pretty looks up and the jewels on her crown shimmer and sparkle.

Cynthia smiles and her kind green eyes meet Damien's. For a few seconds their gazes lock before they both look away, embarrassed.

Mary and Maeve

The church is full to bursting for midnight Mass on this icy cold Christmas Eve.

'Sure, it's desperate out tonight!' exclaims

Father Farwell, rubbing his hands together, as he looks out at the frozen landscape, 'it's pure Baltic, so it is!' He proceeds to drape himself proudly in his white priestly vestments and kisses his embroidered silk stole before placing it carefully over his shoulders. He glances approvingly at his congregants who are filling the pews and smiles with satisfaction. There's Ma Dooley, Maeve and Fearghus McCarthy with their two boys and the divorcee, Mary Rafferty, with a man he hasn't seen before. *Perhaps she's finally found herself a good fella? Well, it's grand to see her back at Mass.*

Maeve adjusts her thick woollen scarf, draping it snugly about her neck, and looks around her. Families are seated together in rows, mammys and daddys and their young children nodding off. *The only one missing is Damien,* she thinks sadly. She resolves to phone him tomorrow and focuses instead on Father Farwell and the choir boys in their red and white robes.

'Aren't the flowers grand?' she whispers to Fearghus, 'Ma Dooley and her team have done a fine job this year.'

'Aye,' says Fearghus, nodding.

She turns her gaze to the nativity scene, encircled with pointsettias in red pots and evergreen garlands threaded with tiny sparkling lights. Candles are flickering, casting shadows against the deep red, burnished wood of the altar stalls and red and green bows are draped around the white marble pillars. Maeve is reminded of

90

her and Mary's First Communion when Damien was an altar boy, solemnly holding the silver platter. Sister Evangelina had instructed the girls to stick out their tongues so that Father Farwell could place the host directly onto them and they'd practised with ice cream wafers. Sister told them that the wafer would actually turn into the body of Christ and it must never, ever, touch their lips or teeth.

'What do we call this, girls?' she'd asked, holding up the wafer between her puffy thumb and forefinger. Maeve had thought that her hands looked like bunches of bananas.

'The host, Sister,' they'd chorused.

'And what does *transubstantiation* mean, girls?'

'The host turns into Jesus' body, Sister.'

'And the wine, girls?'

'Jesus' blood, Sister.'

'And what does Jesus' blood do?'

'It cleanses us from sin, Sister.'

Maeve and Mary had been terrified of the risk of chewing Jesus and had kept their lips shut tight together until the wafer had dissolved, which had made Mary's dimples look like two little craters on either side of her mouth.

Maeve turns to her friend. 'Ah, I do so love Christmas, Mary.'

Mary squeezes her gloved hand and smiles into her honest, open face. *Wholesome. That's what Mammy used to say.* Her cheeks are glowing and her eyes are sparkling with excitement, like an expectant child under the Christmas tree. Seated beside Maeve is Fearghus, his ginger beard reflecting the light from the candles so that it looks like a golden mane, and next to him are young Damien and Brendan.

Such fine young lads, thinks Mary. *Brendan lookin' more and more like his da and young Damien just like his uncle. Sometimes, when I look at his face, it's as though I'm ten years old again, lookin' into the eyes of a teenage Dami. Always so dependable and wise beyond his years* . . . She forces herself to concentrate on the nativity scene in front of her, lest the unwanted memories come slithering back and ambush her.

Maeve smiles at Mary and glances across at Niall, seated beside her. *He's a good fella, so he is. God knows, she could have done worse.* He turns towards her and beams, as he takes Mary's hand in his. Maeve feels a tinge of envy and wishes that Fearghus would take her hand too, but he's never been comfortable with public displays of affection. *He's not even comfortable with private displays either*, she thinks, ruefully. *Never been one to show affection – ah, but he's a good 'un too.*

Maeve and Fearghus had met at 'Youth' which was held every Friday night in the church hall. She and Mary used to call it 'euthanasia'. Mammy had insisted that they go, imagining that they were safe under the watchful eye of Brother Enda, whose name, they discovered, meant 'bird-like'. How they'd laughed at the fact that he did look like a bird, with his long, pointy beak-like nose and little beady eyes. Brother Enda didn't know what was really going on outside in the bushes and in the toilets, especially with Seamus and his gang and was totally out of his depth with hormonal adolescents. But Sister Evangelina had already warned the girls about drugs and sex and teenage boys.

'What are your bodies, girls?'

'They're the temples of the Holy Ghost, Sister.'

'And what do drugs do, girls?'

'They ravage your body, Sister.'

'And do we want to ravage the Holy Ghost's temple, girls?'

'*NOOO,* Sister!'

Fearghus had always been a quiet, reserved, clean-living boy and Maeve had felt safe with him. The fact that Damien approved of him had settled it for her.

Mary

She climbs wearily into bed and pulls the duvet up to her chin. Little flakes of snow are carressing the window panes like feathered crystals, swirling and dancing against the glass.

Outside a blanket of white is spreading over the garden like icing sugar on a cake. She sighs contentedly. It's been a lovely Christmas this year. Midnight Mass with her favourite people beside her and she didn't even feel uncomfortable being back in church, despite Ma Dooley pursing her lips and looking as though she'd just swallowed a lump of faeces. Then Christmas dinner at Maeve's with her delicious roast turkey and trimmings, mince pies and mulled wine . . . and, best of all, dear Niall to share it with her. He'd been so charming and amusing and Mary could tell that Maeve and Fearghus had really liked him and were happy for her and her blossoming relationship. She'd been hugely relieved when she and Niall had finally resolved the issue about her rejection of his kiss, but he hadn't tried to kiss her again. 'Sure, you're a strange one, Mary,' he'd said, 'hidin' secrets inside you. Don't keep me waitin' too long, though. I'm not a priest like yer friend.'

She'd watched Maeve's face when she'd received that phone call and Mary had guessed it was Damien. It had to be Damien. Maeve's face had always lit up when she talked to her brother and she'd giggle and talk too fast. Her cheeks would flush and she'd tuck loose strands of hair behind her ears, like Mammy used to do. But she hadn't alluded to the call and nor had Fearghus.

The past few months leading up to Christmas have been emotionally draining and exhausting for Mary, since her first tentative visit to Dr Lola Paradise, Counselling Psychologist/Family Therapist. Mary had almost cancelled her appointment at the last minute but had resolved that she would give it a go and if she felt in any way uncomfortable, she'd forego any further appointments. She'd been surprised by Dr Paradise's appearance. She was a coffee-coloured American, with a blonde curly wig and a curvaceous body which she celebrated with tight-fitting clothes. Mary had expected her voice to be strident and harsh but instead it was soft and gentle and kind. 'Call me Lola,' she'd said, stretching out her perfectly manicured hand, the bracelets on her wrist jingling, 'come on back, Mary.' She'd ushered her into a little back room with a comfortable sofa and two armchairs with big puffy cushions, a hand-knotted Indian rug on the floor and a vase of bright purple irises on the bookcase. She'd gently questioned Mary about her past, leading her slowly into the dark recesses of her mind, pausing to allow her to weep into a wad of tissues placed strategically beside her.

With the reassuring sound of the clock ticking on the wall behind her and the comforting drone of traffic in the distance, Mary had slowly and hesitantly told Lola about all the losses in her life: about Ma's death when she was four, her childhood with Damien and Maeve, Da's suicide, her abusive relationship with Seamus, the loss of the baby she'd named Grace, Daddy's lingering death and, finally, the greatest loss of all – that of Damien. She'd been shocked and appalled at how easily the tears had come and had just kept on coming, like a river bursting its banks. She'd grabbed at the tissues, blowing her nose noisily, throwing them into the waste bin, grabbing another, until the bin was overflowing and the tissue box was empty. And all the while, Lola had just sat there calmly, watching her with her big, brown, doe eyes, encouraging her in her soft low voice to let it all out.

'Think of your life as a history book, Mary,' she'd said. 'If you tear out the pages that make bad reading there will be gaps and the story won't be entirely true. You need to revisit those pages, re-read them and confront them, however painful it might be.'

In between sobs Mary had talked about Mammy, with her plaited silvery-white hair wound around her head and her weathered rough hands. How she was forever tidying and cleaning, dusting and cooking, rolling out the soda bread dough and then rubbing her floury hands on her apron. Stoical, practical, dependable Mammy who had taken Mary into her bosom, as though she were her own, burying her true feelings deep inside her.

'That's exactly what you've been doing, Mary,' Lola had said, 'denying your feelings and suppressing your emotional energy. You need to confront your pain in order to come through it, to be able to put it behind you.' The light behind Lola had cast a golden glow over the shiny curls of her wig and her smooth brown skin had looked the colour of cinnamon.

She'd recounted to Lola, as though it were yesterday, the sight of Damien's pale face when he'd come into the kitchen after he'd found Da's lifeless body slumped over the steering wheel. How he'd ushered the two girls inside for their tea and had then disappeared, returning a short while later, his face as white as the marble statues of the saints, looking as though all the blood had been drained from it. His eyes had been wide and staring and his hands had been trembling when he'd taken her and Maeve to Ma Dooley next door. When they'd returned to Mammy, he'd sat them down in front of the fire and gently explained that Da had gone.

'Gone? Gone where?' Maeve had shouted, her little face scrunched up in confusion.

'He's gone to Jesus, Maeve.'

'How did he go? Did he drive there? Is he coming back?'

'No, Maeve, he's not coming back. Not ever.'

She'd described to Lola how Maeve had flung herself into Damien's arms and Mammy had slowly removed her apron, staring straight ahead, her lips pressed tightly together as though her mouth was trying to contain something terrible inside it. She'd watched her climb the staircase in slow motion, each step creaking under her broad feet and Mary had just sat there, unmoving, staring into the fire, as the truth sank in. Maeve had no daddy now and she had no mammy. When she'd looked up from the fire into Damien's shocked face, his arms were around Maeve and his hand was gently stroking her, as she sobbed and sobbed into his chest and Mary had believed at that moment that the one person they would always have was Damien. In the safety of Lola's little back room she'd cried and wailed until her nose was red and her eyes were puffy and swollen and she'd felt drained and spent.

Finally, Lola had helped her to say goodbye to the painful memories and to the people who had inhabited them. Under her guidance, she'd recited, 'I accept you as a part of my history and I welcome you back into the book of my life; but I'm also giving you permission to exit my life now.' She'd written their names on pieces of paper which she'd folded carefully and held against her heart. 'You'll always have a place in my heart,' she'd said softly, before letting the papers flutter into the waste bin. When, at last, she'd written Damien's name on the paper and had given him permission to exit her life, she'd cried uncontrollably until she'd felt like she had no more tears left to cry.

She'd returned home feeling shattered and bone-weary and had climbed straight into bed. For the first time in many years she had fallen into a deep sleep and had only woken ten hours later, feeling as though a heavy burden had been lifted from her soul. In the following days she had felt lighter and happier than she had felt in a long while, eager to begin a new chapter in her book of life.

She turns over into a foetal position with her legs curled up underneath her and hugs the pillow against her chest. Rufus nestles into her back, purring, and she drifts off to sleep feeling the comforting, soft, buzzing vibrations humming against her skin.

Damien

He breathes a sigh of relief that Christmas Day has finally passed and with it, all the celebrations. Apart from the last one today at Jerry's home with his neighbours and the walking group and a few other members of his flock. *Only they're not my flock anymore*, he thinks, sadly. *I feel like Judas.*

He parks his battered old Land Rover on the verge of the narrow road outside Jerry's house and is welcomed by three barking dogs and two hissing geese. The smell of chlorine, newly-mown grass and roasting venison greets him as he joins Jerry and his guests around the swimming pool.

'Welcome, Father,' says his host, bowing ceremoniously, before he proceeds to introduce Damien to the other guests: 'Our faithful parish priest, Father Damien.' Jerry is wearing his cloth hat which is starting to fray at the edges. Some of the visitors are staring in fascination at the handsome priest in denims and brown leather 'Jesus sandals' and Damien looks around anxiously for a familiar face. He spots Malcolm, seated beside Dorothy, and sinks gratefully into the empty chair between him and Cynthia. She smiles at Damien and he starts to relax.

Pink gins are served in long glasses filled with tinkling ice cubes and mixed berries. Two huge grey tortoises are lumbering across the manicured lawn, the pool filter is humming quietly in the background and, every few minutes, the *Kreepy Krawly* gasps as it comes up for air. The sky is a clear royal blue, not a cloud in sight, and bonhomie flows amongst the guests, some of whom are wearing bush hats and some wearing Nike caps. Dorothy's face is shielded from the sun by a huge straw hat with a ribbon around it.

These folk are the salt of the earth, thinks Damien, looking around him. Ever since his arrival in this dusty little town ten years ago, they have welcomed him like kin, been family to him. How then will they react when the Bishop announces that Father Damien willl not be returning from his 'sabbatical'? How he wishes that he could have told them himself. He'd pleaded again with the Bishop but he had remained resolute. 'They'll feel that I have betrayed them,' Damien had said angrily, 'I'll look like a craven coward, abandoning them without explanation.'

'Mmmm . . .', the Bishop had replied, 'food for thought, Damien.' He'd insisted it would be better to do it his way and had forbidden Damien to mention the reason for his departure, even to Cynthia and Dorothy. 'We have to follow protocol, I'm afraid. It's a very grave thing when a priest abandons his vocation. A very grave thing indeed.'

Jerry raises his glass in a toast to Father Damien. 'Our faithful parish priest! Good luck on your sabbatical. May the road rise up to meet you and, until we meet again, may God hold you in the palm of His hand.'

Glasses clink and voices chime in unison. 'To Father D!'

Damien blinks back tears and bites his lip. *Faithful parish priest,* he thinks, contemptuously. *Deserter.*

Jerry is onto his third gin and tonic and is rapidly losing his inhibitions. 'I've always admired you priests,' he says, getting on a roll. 'Don't know how you chaps manage to keep a vow of chastity, though. I would have broken that one in a few days!' He giggles nervously, catching his breath, before he takes a long slurp of gin.

'There's a difference between chastity and celibacy, Jerry,' says Malcolm quietly. 'I think you meant a vow of celibacy.' His voice is soft and thin, as though it is not accustomed to being used very often.

'Same thing, surely?' replies Jerry, his face reddening.

'I think not,' says Malcolm. 'I believe it is behoven in the scriptures for us all to be chaste; to be faithful in marriage, to be pure and virtuous.'

Dorothy is staring at Malcolm with undisguised admiration and Cynthia is glancing anxiously at Damien. Silence falls upon the group. Only the hissing of the *Kreepy Krawly* and the gentle sound of a lawnmower in the distance can be heard. Damien takes a sip of his gin and tonic and clears his throat.

'Malcolm is right, Jerry,' he says, choosing his words carefully. 'A vow of celibacy is a promise never to marry, like our Lord and St Paul; chastity, on the other hand, is refraining from a sexual relationship outside of marriage. A priest is married to the church and is called to be

102

an example of Christ.'

Jerry blushes and hastily slugs back the rest of his gin. Mabel Clark, seated beside Cynthia, blanches and wipes her brow with a paper napkin. Dorothy is still staring at Malcolm and Cynthia is staring at her feet. Gradually, ripples of conversation start to erupt again and Damien is no longer the centre of attention. Dorothy and Malcolm are engaged in an intense discussion and Cynthia has been ensnared by Mabel who is wiping her brow again. 'Salacious!' Damien hears her saying, 'my dear, it's just salacious!'

He stands to his feet awkwardly and all eyes turn on him again. 'I must be cracking on,' he says, nodding his head to the group of guests, 'the grace of God on you all.'

Cynthia looks up at him questioningly and Damien raises his hand to her in farewell. Jerry escorts him unsteadily to his vehicle, past the dogs gnawing on huge kudu bones and through the garage, where slabs of raw, red, salted venison are hanging in rows from the ceiling. There are drops of blood on the garage floor and bags of coarse salt lined up against the wall. Jerry proffers his hand.

'Apologies if I spoke out of turn, Father . . .'

'Damien. Just call me Damien, Jerry.' He embraces him in a hug. 'God bless you, man. And thank you for your hospitality. Happiness to you always, Jerry. Happiness to you always.'

He reverses the Land Rover onto the pot-holed street and drives slowly back to the peace and safety of his little red brick house. A battered old taxi with the words *In God we trust* painted across the rear stops abruptly in front of him without warning and he frowns impatiently. He's never been able to get used to the terrible driving habits of the locals, turning without indicating or stopping in the middle of traffic with their hooters blaring for no reason, other than to greet one another.

'No consequences,' he mutters, overtaking the taxi, as a uniformed policeman alights from it. He shakes his head. 'No rules.'

Mary

When she was a little girl, Mary would sometimes hear Daddy crying late at night and she'd crawl into his bed and snuggle up to him. 'Sure, but I miss her, lass,' Frank would sob, 'my mind's too full o' memories.'

Mary doesn't have many memories of Ma, apart from her being ill and hospitalised many times. But she does remember her long, black, braided hair and her kind blue eyes and the feeling of being held in her arms and rocked in the Boston rocker in front of the fire, when Ma was strong enough. She would sing in her soft, frail voice, 'Too-ra-loo-ra-too-ral, hush now, don't you cry,' and Mary would drift off to sleep. One picture that still stands out clearly in her mind is of Ma confined to her wheelchair, gazing wistfully through the window at the passing traffic and the green fields beyond.

Daddy didn't know how to brush Mary's thick curly hair and tie it into a ponytail and he also didn't know when or how to buy Mary a bra. So Mammy had taken the girls to Patrick Street and bought them little white cotton bras that were like triangles of fabric that covered their nipples. Size 28AA. She and Maeve had been hugely relieved to join the group of bra wearers because some of the older girls at school would run their fingers down the spines of the younger girls and laugh at them if they didn't feel the strip of elastic across their backs which elevated them from the ranks of children to teenagers. The little white bras had gradually turned grey and, when the girls were sixteen, Mammy had let them choose their own bras; but never black lacy ones like Rosheen Murphy's. Mary used to wonder if the nuns had breasts and if they wore bras because their chests looked so flat; except for Sister Evangelina's chest. Mary thought she looked like a pillow with a belt tied around it.

She still remembers the day when she was twelve and had started bleeding and Damien had found her crying in the bicycle shed. 'Ah, Mary, look at you there!' he'd exclaimed, putting his arms around her and wiping her face with his shirt sleeve. 'What is it, lass? Are you hurt?' Between sobs, she'd told him that she was dying. 'I'm bleedin' like the sacred heart of Jesus,' she'd cried, 'I'm goin' to die and leave Daddy all alone!' His face had flushed and he'd told her to ask Mammy to explain what was happening to her. 'Mammy knows, Mary. You're not goin' to die. You're just becomin' a woman now.'

Mammy had put her hands on Mary's shoulders and looked squarely into her huge, terrified eyes. 'God love ya, Mary. Tis only the bleedin' yer havin'. The monthlies. The curse.' Mary had been none the wiser but she didn't like the idea of having a curse. Mammy had sent her and Maeve to Mr Patel's to buy sanitary towels and Damien had bought them a book called *A Girl's Guide to Growing Up*. She and Maeve had read it in her bedroom, giggling at the pictures and the description of them changing from 'little girls to grown-up women'. They'd practised trying to say the word 'vagina' and pronounced it *vajeena*. Damien had overheard them and had corrected their pronunciation, warning them not to say the word, especially in front of Mammy.

When they were eleven, Mrs Boyle, the Biology teacher, had been elected to give the class a lesson on sex and reproduction and she'd told them that some girls would grow breasts like grapes and some would be like watermelons. Mary and Maeve had prayed that they wouldn't grow watermelons like Ma Dooley's. Poor Daddy had been ill-equipped to deal with the subject of the birds and the bees and Sister Evangelina had put the fear of God into them concerning chastity, purity and eternal damnation.

'What is the gravest kind of sin, girls?'

'Sexual sin, Sister.'

'And what does it do to your soul, girls?'

'Threatens it with eternal damnation, Sister.'

'We're all called to chastity, girls. Remember that.'

'What's chastity, Sister?' Mary had asked.

'I know! I know!' Maeve had shouted, waving her hand in the air, 'it's bein' pure.'

They didn't really understand what being pure meant or what sexual sin was, nor did they understand the meaning of eternal damnation. Only Rosheen Murphy didn't seem too concerned about sin and damnation or the fact that she was referred to as 'The Slag'.

Damien

Damien trundles along the bumpy road in his Land Rover, his thoughts returning to the conversation he'd had with Maeve the previous day.

He'd just returned home after saying Mass and shaking hands with the usual visitors who always appear out of nowhere on Christmas day, greeting his flock and sharing mince pies and Dorothy's warm mulled wine with them. He'd struggled to prepare a sermon for that morning service, and had felt drained and exhausted when he was finally released from the jollity and could wipe the false smile from his face and go home. Home to his little red brick house with its baking verandah and wilting flower beds. Home to no one. He had settled down at the old pine kitchen table to eat his Christmas lunch of leftovers from Cynthia's party, when the phone had rung. He'd impatiently brushed away a fly that was about to settle on the succulent pink ham and popped a glazed cherry into his mouth before answering.

'Father Damien,' he'd said, rather irritably.

'Dami!' cried Maeve, 'it's me! Happy Christmas!'

'Ah, Maeve, love!' he'd responded, the frown on his face turning into a smile, 'sure, it's good to hear your voice again.'

He had pictured her and Fearghus with the boys, gathered around the fire in their cosy front room, the Christmas tree aglow with baubles and fairy lights and the table laden with turkey and glazed ham, Brussels sprouts and carrots and her crisp roast potatoes and parsnips. And Mammy's 'Christmas gravy'.

'It's desperate out!' Maeve had exclaimed, 'absolutely bitter! You wouldn't put the dog out! And it's goin' to get worse. D'ya remember back when we had the big snow, Dami?' She'd rattled on, words tumbling out disjointedly, with Damien interjecting every once in a while. 'Will you be comin' home for the reunion, then, Dami? It would be grand to see you again . . . the boys are gettin' so big, you won't recognise 'em!' He'd spoken to Fearghus and the two boys and had intimated that he would be taking a sabbatical soon. Not the right time to tell them the truth, he'd decided. He'd thought he could hear other voices in the background but Maeve hadn't mentioned having visitors.

He parks outside the house and goes straight to the bedroom where he disrobes and pulls on an old T-shirt and a pair of shorts before making a sandwich and pouring himself a stiff whiskey. He eats aimlessly at the kitchen table then takes his plate to the sink, runs the hot tap over it and places it on the drying rack next to the single coffee mug and glass. *The evidence of a solitary man*, he thinks, wistfully. He makes his way to the verandah, clutching his re-filled wine glass and a mince pie wrapped in a red paper napkin, settles into the chair and opens the gift that Cynthia had given him on Christmas Eve. It's an expensive pale blue cashmere sweater, as soft and delicate as lamb's wool. He runs his fingers over it and holds it against his cheek; he's never before owned such an expensive garment. He reaches for his sellotaped reading spectacles, opens the attached card and starts to read.

My dear Damien,

I don't know where to start, how to put into words what I feel, now that you are leaving. (And I know that you are leaving and not just taking a leave of absence.) I don't think you are aware of how many lives you have changed in the time you have been our parish priest – mine most of all. You have shown us what a real man is, what true kindness looks like, generosity, compassion, patience . . . I could go on and on but most of all, you have shown me God. A merciful God who loves me unconditionally and who will comfort me when you have gone. I have always known that there is a deep sadness in your soul, a loss that you could never share and I pray that you will find the key to unlocking the pain and finally know that you are home.

With my love always, Cynthia

For several minutes he sits motionless, staring into the horizon, seeing nothing. *Most of all you have shown me God.* Hot tears are pouring down his cheeks, soaking his shirt, causing the ink on the card to run into black streaks. His chest heaves as he weeps over what he is about to lose and the irony that the very qualities he had thought he lacked and which disqualified him as a priest, were the very qualities that Cynthia had recognised in him. He breathes a deep, juddering sigh as the tears subside, then closes the card and slips it into his Bible. He wipes his eyes with the paper napkin, swallows the mince pie absentmindedly in two bites and steps out into the now shady garden.

When Damien was a lad of ten, Da took the family to a botanical garden for tea. He and the girls had run loose through the shady ferns and hedges and small trees, along the pathways and over the stepping stones, before collapsing, breathless, into the thick deep piles of fallen leaves. There were little humpbacked bridges spanning ponds surrounded by grasses and irises and white water lilies with pink edges floating serenely on the still water which had looked almost purple in the reflecting light. The lilies were just like the ones in the picture in Mammy's bedroom of Monet's *Water Lily Pond* and Damien had felt such peace and contentment, he'd wished that he could live in that garden forever, imagining himself floating over the pond like a butterfly, or soaring free like a bird in the clear blue sky. They'd discovered a Koi fish pond in one corner of the garden and Maeve and Mary had been terrified at the sight of the huge colourful fish. When they'd finally joined Da and Mammy for milkshakes, Maeve had said excitedly, spreading her arms out wide, 'we saw a humongous goldfish!' Da had puffed on his pipe, before explaining to Maeve that it was a Koi. 'It's a Japanese fish, darlin'. A Dragon Koi fish. Legend has it that those fish that could swim upstream and pass the dragon's gate would turn into powerful dragons.'

Maeve's eyes had been like two saucers. 'Are dragons real, Da?'

'No, darlin', they're mythical creatures, like unicorns,' Da had replied, tapping his pipe against the chair leg.

'I've seen one in a book about St George slayin' a dragon!' Mary had interjected,

112

breathlessly, 'they have wings like bats and scaly tails and they breathe fire!'

'A legend, Mary, lass. Just a story, my girl,' Da had said, blowing smoke rings into the air, 'but a Komodo dragon on the other hand . . .'

'Enough now, Albert!' Mammy had interjected, 'you'll be scarin' the bejaysus out o'them.' She'd forked a large piece of lemon meringue pie into her mouth and Damien had wondered if, perhaps, the creamy yellow custard and stiff, golden-brown meringue might taste better than his chocolate cake. *Ah, life was so uncomplicated then.*

He settles himself onto the old wood and iron bench under the jacaranda tree, savouring the stillness and the almost tangible silence. The heat is making mirages on the dimpled tarmac road and there are shallow, muddy puddles on the driveway after the rain the night before.

He closes his eyes and imagines that he's in the botanical garden again with Maeve and Mary, listening to the sound of gently lapping water and birdsong and smelling the exotic fragrance of jasmine and water lilies and gardenias. He was happy then.

Maeve

Maeve hastens along the little bridge, her hair blowing back in the gust of wind that has appeared out of nowhere. She can hardly contain her excitement, now that the day has finally arrived when she'll be seeing her beloved brother again. Once she gets home, she'll bake some of Damien's favourite soda bread – Mammy's recipe that has never been known to fail.

She pauses and leans over the parapet. The waters of the brook have settled and she can see her reflection on the still surface and the flat round stones on the bottom. Memories of her and Mary leaning over the bridge on their way home from school come flooding back: the girls staring at their blurry faces in the mirror-like surface of the freezing water in winter and Damien skimming pebbles across the stream in summer. The flat stones would dance across the water, leaving rippled circles behind, until their images disappeared. He'd soon get bored and would chivvy them up. 'Race you to Flannagans!' he'd shout and they'd run, shrieking behind him with their satchels swinging from their backs.

A fish jumps and startles her out of her reverie. She notices a few clusters of white water lilies floating on the slow-moving water at the edge of the stream, their golden-yellow stamens pointing up to the sun like little crowns. They remind her of the pond at the botanical garden where Da took them for tea. She remembers sitting on a bench between Damien and Mary, watching tiny black beetles whizzing over the surface of the pond and dragon flies swooping like little helicopters over the lilies and she recalls a feeling of deep contentment. She remembers, too, running through the park with Damien and Mary and having huge slices of chocolate cake and strawberry milkshakes under a big garden umbrella with Mammy and Da. Dear Da, puffing on his pipe, and Mammy tucking into her lemon meringue pie . . .

She lingers for a few more minutes, her eyes following the path that led to their secret place under the oak tree where they used to lie in their shorts in summer. Her skin would always be covered in freckles by the end of summer but they'd fade in the winter months. She shudders, remembering what she and Mary had seen there all those years ago and hurries on.

Images flash before her as she passes Mr Patel's shop with that horrible elephant god statue and the smell of incense and spices: little ginger-haired Ronnie Watson being teased as he dragged his lame leg behind him, while Seamus and his gang threw conkers at him, calling him a 'coppernob capper'. Maeve had never seen Damien so angry, as he threw down his bag of books and Seamus in the jaw so hard, it had sent him reeling back into Mr Patel's vegetable display. Mr Patel had come running out of his shop, shouting, 'Feck off, y'all, feckin'eejits! I'll call the guards on y'all now!' His wife, Fatima, had started shouting in Hindi, waving her arms in the air, howling like a banshee, and Maeve remembers the crimson blood spurting from Seamus' face and the lacerations on Damien's bloodied hand. He'd carried a sobbing Ronnie home on his back and the little boy's eyes had been wide with terror. When they'd reached Ma Watson's house she was already waiting anxiously outside, wearing a bright green, hand-knitted cardigan, rubbing her hands on her apron.

'Look at the state o' you, Ronnie!' she'd cried, as Damien had explained what had happened, 'and yer hand is bleedin', Damien, son. That Seamus is a scum bastard to be sure.

Feckin' eejit. Face like a smacked arse!' She'd ushered them into her shabby little house and made them hot cocoa in mugs with the Queen's face on them, then she'd cleaned Damien's hand with Dettol. Maeve had never seen so many statues of saints and pictures of The Blessed Virgin holding the baby Jesus, and The Sacred Heart of Jesus with blood dripping from it, like the blood dripping from Seamus' face. Little red lights were burning under the statues, like the ones at the Convent, and she'd felt nervous and anxious. She'd never been so relieved to get out into the fresh air again and go home to Mammy.

She'd refused to go into Mr Patel's shop ever again after he'd acquired the carved wooden statue of the beady-eyed Hindu elephant god, Lord Ganesha. Its huge belly, broken tusk and four hands (two of them waving a whip and an axe) had traumatised her. Sister Evangelina had told them that a Madonna statue in Italy had actually been weeping blood. (*Why is it always blood?* Maeve had wondered.) She'd told Da that evening, in shocked tones, when they were seated at the dining table but he had dismissed the story with contempt.

'Ah, Maeve, darlin', that nun is talkin' a load o' baloney! That 'blood' was found to be of human male origin and, if I'm not mistaken, the owner of the statue refused to take a DNA test.'

'There she goes again, Albert!' Mammy had

cried, thumping the table. 'That nun! Puttin' the fear of God into those poor wee lasses.'

'What's a DNA test?' Maeve had asked.

'Just eat yer dinner now, Maeve,' Mammy had said, exasperated. 'Questions, questions. Always questions.'

'Och, Agnes,' Da had scolded, ''tis a fine thing for a wean to be questionin'.'

Maeve had never been able to understand how anyone could find comfort from a cold, lifeless statue of The Blessed Mother or a picture of Jesus and His bleeding heart in their home. They had lovely pictures of flowers and water lilies in their house.

After Damien had punched Seamus, little Ronnie Watson had waited every day for him and the girls to pass on their way to school and had limped along beside them, looking up at Damien's face with undisguised admiration. Maeve had never felt so proud, as she did then, that Damien was her brother. Seamus had kept away from him after that day, biding his time until he could finally inflict the ultimate act of retribution by stealing the love of Damien's life.

Damien

He looks around the room one last time and closes his battered suitcase. Not much to show for the last ten years. A transparent ginger gheko slips behind the curtain and a black millipede, or *chongololo* as the locals call it, slowly makes its way alongside the skirting board, its burnt orange legs waving like fields of wheat. They'd laughed at him when he'd first arrived and had been afraid of the harmless creatures and he'd had to learn which spiders and snakes were dangerous and how to hang a mosquito net over his bed during the rainy season.

There is so much about Africa he'll miss: the vibrant colours, the bright early sunrises, the striking sunsets and the smell of rain and woodsmoke; the salty taste of *biltong,* the raw venison with a moist red centre and hard dry outer crust, cut into slithers and washed down with an ice cold beer; and his favourite meal of white stodgy porridge made from maize meal,

119

which the locals call *sadza*, dipped in relish and eaten with bare hands. And the birdsong. He'll miss the birdsong. Jerry has taught him to identify the *glug-glug* sound of the coucal, or 'bottle bird', the *ka-ka* of the red-billed hornbill and the liquid trilling of the Heuglins robin ('the best singer in the world, bloody marvellous!')

He looks out at the dry wilting garden. His lovingly-planted hanging baskets are starting to droop in the relentless heat and the once green lawn is now covered with patches of dead brown grass. Living in Africa has taught him the value of water. Never again will he complain about the relentless rain in Ireland. *Who will come after me?* he wonders, for it must be a he. *Will he take care of what little garden is left?*

Gardening has become an activity of pleasure now, not a means of escaping from the reality of his old life. Since making that momentous decision to leave the priesthood, he feels as though he can breathe at last. No longer Father Damien, struggling to be the perfect priest to merit his salvation. No more clerical garb and listening to endless confessions, pronouncing absolution as though he, himself, was God. A simple life of teaching and counselling, pottering in the garden and spending time with Maeve and the boys is all he wishes for now and he's excited at the prospect of beginning a new chapter in his life. There's the possibility of a position as head of English at his old school, or of becoming a family therapist. He still hasn't told Maeve that he's left the priesthood. She never could understand, anyway, why he chose a life of self-denial and sacrifice but plenty of time to explain . . . all the time in the world now.

He pulls on his worn old jacket, grabs the handle of his suitcase and heaves it off the bed, then checks one last time that he has his passport and ticket before closing the front door of the little house that has been his home for the last ten years. He pauses on the steaming verandah, inhaling the pungent smell of Cobra floor polish and the faint aroma of jasmine. On the faded brick wall are a few dark squares and rectangles where the pictures of the walking group used to hang; he's packed them carefully in his suitcase. For the first time he notices a long tear in the sun-bleached calico blind. The seat of the shabby old Parker Knoll chair is sagging and there's a white circular stain on the coffee table. How many hours and days and years has he spent sitting on that chair, looking out at his garden, drinking coffee while the sun was rising before the heat of the day had begun to settle over everything like a heavy blanket? How many sermons has he prepared, seated on that chair with Da's Bible beside him? And how many nights has he sat alone in the darkness, drinking whiskey, while listening to Beethoven and thinking about the people and places he loved? The people who have stayed in his heart but not in his life. And the one person he has never stopped loving, whose memory has haunted him since he left Ireland.

He steps into the driveway just as Dorothy pulls up in her little white Honda.

Dorothy

Dorothy has been looking forward to having Father D all to herself, even though it means saying goodbye to him at the end of the journey. There are many things she would like to say to him but she fears that she may not have the courage to verbalise them, so she's written them in a card. She's gone to a bit of trouble with her appearance, as she'd like Father D to remember her with fondness and approval. She's even sprayed some *Chanel No 5* behind her ears, as she'd like her smell to linger after she's hugged Father D goodbye. She only uses perfume on special occasions and this is a very special occasion.

From the moment she first met Father D she has been in love with him. Oh, she knows that she can never have him, not in that base physical sense, but in a far deeper, soulish, spiritual union. They have so much in common, after all: the love of music, poetry and literature to start with. She's seen him watching her play the organ with a look of pure joy on his face and she's sure that he too can feel that unspoken bond they share. She'll miss him terribly but she understands how much he needs this break from the parish – he is human, after all. She feels a little flutter of excitement as she pulls up at the rectory and sees him waiting outside with his old battered suitcase. He's wearing one of her shirts under his jacket and this pleases her immensely. She opens the boot and the passenger door and he climbs in. She hopes he can smell her perfume.

'This is very kind of you, Dorothy,' he says, pushing the seat back to accommodate his long legs. She's always loved his Irish accent and his deep, melodious voice.

'No *problemo*, Father,' she says, glancing in the rearview mirror, 'I'm honoured to be the one to see you on your way.' She clutches the steering wheel with both her hands and glances anxiously at the speedometer. She wouldn't want Father to be shocked by her careless driving.

Damien glances through the window at the rusted and broken signposts on the potholed road and the overgrown verges. Raw sewage water is seeping from a blocked drain and barefoot children are wading through it, laughing as they splash each other, their white teeth flashing in their chocolate brown faces. They wave at the passing car and Dorothy parps the hooter. Damien smiles as they pass the familiar sign announcing, *Circumcision done at eye clinic,* displayed crookedly on the lamp post by the turnoff to Cynthia's house. He would have preferred to have her take him to the airport but perhaps it's for the best; he may not have been able to hide the truth from her.

They'd said their final goodbyes the night before after he'd had supper with her under the gazebo by the pool. They'd chatted about the weather, about some of the hikes they'd had together, about Ireland and about Cynthia's daughter, Emma, but there'd been a slight tension in the air, an unspoken awareness of unexpressed thoughts and feelings. When he'd finally stood up to leave she'd hesitated, before wrapping her arms around him and hugging him closely. He'd recognised her scent immediately – *Anais Anais,* the perfume Da had given Mammy for her birthday in the pink and white bottle which she'd proudly displayed on her dressing table. It smelt of hyacinths and talcum powder and Maeve and Mary used to squirt it behind their ears when Mammy wasn't looking. They called it *Anus Anus.* Mammy stopped using it after Da died but Damien had smelled it on her again when Frank started going to the Bingo with her.

'You will keep in touch, now, won't you?' Cynthia had whispered. 'Perhaps I'll take a holiday and come and visit you in Ireland?'

'Sure, that would be grand, Cynthia,' Damien had replied, kissing her softly on her cheek, trying not to think about how much he would miss her. She'd stood at the gate, a sad figure waving goodbye, and he'd wanted to turn around and go back to her one last time and tell her that he was no longer a priest.

He and Dorothy talk about the weather and the prospect of more rain. He thanks her again for her regular musical accompaniment at Mass and compliments her skill on the organ. They talk about the other parishioners, including Malcolm, and Damien is relieved when Dorothy says shyly, 'I always thought he was pompous and boring, but he's not, he's actually not.'

'No,' says Damien, 'he's a good man, Malcolm. A good man.'

Dorothy is squinting into the sun and her face has a sheen of perspiration over it. She's leaning forward over the steering wheel and rubbing her thumbs back and forth; her knuckles look prominent and white and her nails are chewed to the quick. Her intense perfume is cloying and Damien longs to open the window and thrust his head into the fresh air. He focuses on the jacaranda trees which have started losing their blossoms, covering the road with a thick purple carpet. 'Beautiful sight,' he says, 'I'm gonna miss it.'

Dorothy nods and smiles. She wishes she could think of something intelligent to say in reply but she suddenly feels tongue-tied and is afraid that her voice might sound feeble. They sit in silence as she stares at the road straight ahead.

Damien watches the town gradually diminishing until the houses are replaced by mealie fields which then fade into dry bushveld. They pass the newly-built Catholic mission with its facebrick buildings and water tanks and generators. The yard is bare and barren and there is no sign of life, like the new Chinese-built medical centre in town with a huge padlock on the gate and the half-built, abandoned university. Dorothy sticks doggedly to the speed limit and they crawl along behind a bus which is belching smoke and teetering dangerously to one side. Piled on the roof rack are suitcases, bicycles, large boxes and petrified, caged chickens, their red combs blowing back in the wind.

'I sure am glad I'm not on that bus, Dorothy,' says Damien. 'Poor souls – they must have nerves of steel.'

Dorothy nods, wiping her brow with the back of her hand. 'You have to have your wits about you with these buses; they're a law unto themselves,' she mutters, nervously, as she accelerates past the bus in a cloud of smoke. She slows down again, glancing anxiously at the speedometer, her eyes darting from the rearview mirror to the wing mirror, fearful that she might miss her blind spot. At last they pull up at the new Chinese-built airport. Dorothy shyly hands Damien a white envelope, before throwing her arms around him and weeping softly into his shoulder. He pats her gently before prising himself from her grasp.

'God bless you, Dorothy, lass,' he says, 'I'm indebted to you for your kindness. You're a fine, strong woman, an asset to the church. Look after Malcolm now – he needs your support.'

She watches Father D make his way to the departure lounge, his long legs striding in front of the old battered suitcase he's dragging behind him. His jacket is old-fashioned and worn, like his sellotaped, tortoise-shell reading specs and he seems out-of-place in his surroundings. She wants to run after him and tell him how much she loves him and how much she'll miss him. Instead, she wipes away her tears and climbs back behind the wheel, feeling deflated and empty.

She has a strange feeling that Father D may never be coming back.

Damien

He settles into his window seat, buckles the seat belt and looks out at the dry savanna bushveld and the rows of acacia trees on the far edge of the landing strip. They seem to be quivering and vibrating in the shimmering heat, reflecting a subdued, tremulous light. He watches the landscape gradually diappear as the plane soars into the cloudless blue sky, far above the long straight road that led back to the town he'd called home and the folk he'd called family. 'Goodbye,' he whispers, closing his eyes and blinking back the tears. What was that African proverb? *The eye never forgets what the heart has seen.* He takes his specs from his pocket, opens Dorothy's card and starts to read.

Dear Father D,

I would like to wish you well on your journey and to thank you for the blessing you have been to me and our parish. All I can say is that you are the most Christ-like man I have ever met and I will miss you terribly. Have a wonderful, well-deserved sabbatical.

With love and best wishes.
God bless you,
Dorothy

Christ-like, he muses, shaking his head. *Me? Christ-like?* He thinks about the good, proud, honest folk he's left behind and how they'd always 'make a plan' when problems arose, sharing what little they had, even during times of famine and shortages. His thoughts turn to Jerry with his passion for the African bushveld and his knowledge of indigenous flora and fauna and birdlife. *He'll be a fine leader for the walking group, keep it going . . . be good for Malcolm and Dorothy. No, maybe not Dorothy.* He pictures her flushed face and large, cumbersome body, her heavy feet pressing down the pedals as she threw herself at the organ. *Ah, but she has a good heart.* Finally, he thinks of Cynthia. Their parting had been the most difficult. She'd always seemed to understand him, to see him as a man and not only as a priest. She'd known that he had been attracted to her in a way that a priest should not be and he'd known that she was fond of him too . . . more than fond. Perhaps she loved him? But that kind of love had been denied to Father Damien. Until now. And all he knows about love is heartbreak and betrayal and a terrible wound in his heart that has never healed.

Far below, the sepia colours of ochre and brown are blending into a patchwork of squares and triangles interspersed with strips of olive green and blue. He forces himself to think instead of the breathtaking beauty and green fields of his homeland. *Tomorrow I'll be lookin' out at a different landscape . . .*

He leans back and closes his eyes. *What did our Lord say? Take therefore no thought for the morrow, for the morrow shall take thought for the things of itself.* 15

Maeve

Maeve is bursting with excitement at the thought of seeing her brother again. 'I'm delira and excira!' she tells Fearghus on the way to the airport. 'Of course, it would be bucketin' down though, wouldn't it? Nice welcome for Dami.'

Fearghus parks in the open parking area and they hasten to International Arrivals, where they glance anxiously at the board above them.

'He's almost landed, Fearghus!' Maeve cries.

'Calm down, will you, lass?' says Fearghus, 'he'll be here any minute.'

'Oh, I can hardly contain m'self!' she cries, clasping her hands together.

The aircraft descends over the dark blue sea and the bay that looks purple in the light reflected over the water. On the horizon is a crimson line, blending into orange, then yellow and finally pink. As the plane approaches the runway, emerald green fields come into focus with patches of yellow and mauve peeping behind heavy grey clouds. Passengers wait impatiently to disembark until, finally, the doors are opened and Damien steps down the aircraft steps into lashing rain. He proceeds on the long, cold walk to the airport building, crosses a soaking ramp and climbs the stairs of an airbridge, emerging into the brightly lit terminal. He looks around at the sea of faces and there, standing behind a barrier, are Maeve and Fearghus, waving and smiling.

'Ah, is it not yerself, Damien?' laughs Fearghus, enveloping him in a bear hug.

Maeve embraces him warmly, pressing her face against his chest, her arms wrapped tightly around his neck. She squeezes his shoulders and steps back, glancing at his old suitcase and worn jacket. 'Look at you there, Dami!' she exclaims, 'we'll have to be takin' you down Patrick Street . . . kit you out like a modern fella. You look like a culchie! Need a good haircut too!' She hugs him again. 'Ah, but I've missed you so, Dami. It's grand to have you home again.'

When she'd seen her brother emerge through the sliding glass doors, with his damp messy hair in disarray and a shadow of dark stubble on his face, she'd wanted to leap over the barrier and run into his arms. She'd felt a surge of pride and tenderness towards him: this modest, unassuming man who had given up so much to help others, denying his own happiness in the process. He'd never have spent his meagre stipend on himself or on items that he would have considered extravagances and he'd have given his last penny to help someone in need, depriving himself instead. She'd wanted to weep at the sight of his old battered suitcase and outdated jacket, incongruous with the expensive-looking, pale-blue cashmere jumper he was wearing underneath it.

She looks up at his handsome, tanned, slightly-weathered face, her rosy cheeks flushed with excitement, and links her arm in his as they step out into the cold wet car park.

'Ah, it's grand to see you again, Dami,' she sighs happily, 'it's been so long.'

'Aye, Maeve,' says her brother, inhaling the sweet, earthy, musky smell of the rain, 'it's been too long.'

Mary

The weather is turning at last and the yellow creeping buttercups are in full bloom, their bright golden faces reaching up to the sun. Peeping through the shady hedgerows and grassy roadside banks are pink-red campions and, in the fields beyond, deep violet-blue salvia with their wrinkly sage-green leaves and reddish-brown wild cherry trees covered in pretty white flowers. Their sweet gentle fragrance wafts in the heavy humid air as Mary pedals along the lane, humming quietly, loose tendrils escaping from the chignon she'd fastened that morning. Her cheeks are glowing with perspiration and there's a faint sheen above her cherry red lips. She's been wearing lipstick every day lately and has been spraying *Anais Anais* behind her ears, like Mammy used to do. She's wearing a white peasant, off-the-shoulder blouse and a blue chiffon skirt which is billowing behind her. Since her weekly therapy sessions with Lola and the re-kindling of her relationship with Niall, she's been feeling at one with the world, full of renewed energy and a *joie de vivre* she hasn't experienced for years. The past is behind her and the future is full of promise.

When she was a child the things she had hoped for were simple: jelly and custard for dessert, chocolate after dinner and longer daylight hours so that she and Maeve could stay outside riding their bicycles. She'd hoped for the rain to stop, or for Ma to get better and, as she got older, she'd hoped that she'd passed her exams and that the holidays would come soon so that she could spend more time with Damien. Her hopes then were just glimmers of possibilities, some feel-good moments which would one day become pleasant memories but now she feels something more than hope – she feels optimism and excitement at the prospect of a new beginning with Niall.

She's about to take the turn-off to her cottage but decides instead to pop in and see Maeve; she's been too busy lately to visit her old friend but it's Friday today and school is out. She dismounts at the front door, smoothes her hair and adjusts her skirt, before ringing the doorbell. 'Anyone home?' she calls.

She can hear footsteps coming from the kitchen. The door opens suddenly and there, standing before her, outlined in the portal, is Damien. Her hands fly to her face and she stares in disbelief. 'Oh, my God . . . oh, my God,' she whispers, as the colour drains from her face.

'Who is it, Dami?' calls Maeve from the kitchen.

Mary wants to run, to escape, to be anywhere else but here, at the same time feeling helplessly drawn towards the dear familiar figure in front of her. They both stand in shock, unable to speak, until Maeve calls from the hall.

'C'mon inside, Mary.'

She glances anxiously at her friend's ashen face, ushering her into the sitting room, as she starts chattering about nothing, her eyes darting from Damien to Mary.

'You didn't tell me, Maeve Why didn't you tell me?' Mary starts wringing her hands, running them through her hair, smoothing down her skirt, adjusting her blouse, pressing her lips tightly together.

Maeve puts her head in her hands. 'I'm sorry, Mary, my love, I'm so sorry. I thought it was for the better. Here, take a seat . . .' She turns to Damien, her eyes wide and questioning.

'Shall I be wettin' the tea, then?' he says, turning towards the kitchen.

The front door flies open and Fearghus and the boys barge in, sweaty and breathless after their run.

'Thought it was your bike outside, young Mary. What a nice surprise!' says Fearghus, wiping his face with his sleeve. 'Haven't see you in donkeys. Been otherwise occupied, then?'

'Tea is the only thing for this heat!' blurts Maeve, hurrying to the kitchen, making clucking noises. Hushed voices and whispering can be heard through the open door and Damien returns, carrying the tea tray. He places it on the coffee table and takes a seat at the bay window. The boys engage Mary in a conversation about school and soccer and university choices and Fearghus comments on the state of the economy and the recent fine weather. Finally the chatter abates and the room becomes quiet.

'It's awful warm now!' exclaims Maeve, breaking the silence. She glances anxiously at Damien and then at Mary, who is sitting on the edge of her seat as though she is frozen. 'I'm not able for this heat at all.'

'God, I tell you, I'm sweatin' like a bullock,' says Fearghus, getting to his feet. 'It's cruel warm out there. I'm goin' for a quick shower . . . boys, why not leg it down to Patel's and get us a block of ice cream?' He hands them a ten pound note and playfully flicks a dishcloth at them, 'and don't forget the feckin' wafers this time!'

The boys excuse themselves and Maeve leaps up and removes the tea tray before bustling to the kitchen and closing the door. A tangible silence fills the room. Damien turns to Mary who is clasping her hands anxiously and looking at the floor.

'I thought you'd left the village,' he says, 'Maeve didn't tell me you were still here.'

She looks up and flushes. 'No, I'm still here,' she says, 'still teachin' at the Convent, livin' in Daddy's cottage . . . '

'Yer looking good. Haven't aged much in twenty years.'

She smiles. 'You're lookin' good, too, Dami. A bit older and greyer, but . . . '

They both laugh nervously. She leans back into a cushion and tucks a loose strand of hair behind her ear.

'Are you happy out in Africa? I can see that it suits you. Nice and tanned. Bet you don't miss the Irish weather?'

Damien looks thoughtful. 'I do – sometimes. When the day dawns sweltering hot (worse than today) and it's still sweltering at night until, finally, the pressure breaks and the heavens open and you just want to run outside and stand in the pouring rain.' He pauses. 'Hard to imagine here.'

Mary isn't listening anymore. She's watching his mouth move, observing the deep lines etched across his forehead and on either side of his lips, the silver-grey hair at his temples and his tanned golden skin. His muscles seem bigger, his whole body seems bigger, and he has a commanding presence that makes her unable to look away. *What a beautiful priest you are, Father Damien,* she thinks. She forces herself to look away and then turns back. Their eyes lock and she looks away again, her cheeks flushing. She gets quickly to her feet.

'I must be crackin' on,' she says, her voice sounding thin and tremulous, 'lots to do.'

'Mary,' says Damien, softly, 'we need to talk. Tomorrow?'

She nods. 'Tomorrow. Supper?'

Damien

When he'd opened the door and seen Mary standing there Damien had felt as though his heart had suddenly stopped beating. That same thick black hair tumbling around her face, the loose tendrils curling softly down her neck; her slim, lithe body with her smooth, creamy shoulders framed by the elastic of her blouse; her huge blue eyes and her full red lips. He'd felt as though he was drowning and had wanted to envelop her in his arms, when Maeve had called over his shoulder and had ushered them in.

Hours later, sitting on his bed, he re-lives every moment of that visit.

The conversation had been stilted and awkward at first but he couldn't take his eyes off Mary and, whenever she glanced up she would look straight into his eyes. Why hadn't Maeve warned him? Why hadn't she told him that Mary was still here, living in Frank's old cottage, teaching at the Convent? That she'd never remarried, never had a child of her own?

He stares out at the inky night sky, suspended like a black velvet blanket freckled with stars. The same sky they used to lie under so long ago, trying to identify Venus, Jupiter and Mars. So many years have passed, so much water under the bridge, but now it's time . . . time to put the past to rest. He'll go to the cottage tomorrow night and make his peace with Mary.

He starts to undress, folding his clothes neatly over the chair back, then slips under the crisp, lavender-scented sheets. Their evocative scent reminds him of Miss O'Leary. He reaches for his tortoise-shell reading glasses and opens his book.

Tell me, what else should I have done?
Doesn't everything die at last, and too soon?
Tell me, what is it you plan to do
With your one wild and precious life? 16

He pauses, meditating on the words. *So, what is it you plan to do now, Damien? Will you waste another twenty years denying yourself, denying your pain?*

He pictures Miss O'Leary standing in front of the class, twisting her lace handkerchief. 'T S Eliot said dat *poo-etry* is not a turnin' loose of emotions but an escape *from* emotions,' she'd said earnestly, 'and only dose who have personality and emotions know what it means to want to escape dem.' She'd stopped and looked straight into Damien's eyes.

Is that what I've been tryin' to do all these years? Is that why I joined the priesthood? To escape my emotions?

When he was working in the book shop after Da died, Damien discovered a copy of *Either/Or: A Fragment of Life,* by Soren Kierkegaard, the philosopher Da used to quote. He'd carefully turned the pages of the heavy tome with its dark, melancholic cover and had become engrossed in the philosopher's words. *What is a poet?* he'd read. *An unhappy person who conceals profound anguish in his heart, but whose lips are so formed that as sighs and cries pass over them, they sound like beautiful music.* Damien had agreed with those sentiments – he was an unhappy person, concealing profound anguish in his heart. He'd continued reading: *My inwardness is too true for me to be able to talk about it.* Damien had concurred with that sentiment entirely; he still could not share those deep private thoughts and feelings that he expressed in his poems, not even with Mary.

He closes the book and switches off the bedside light. Sleep evades him, as thoughts of Mary flood his mind. He cannot deny that, apart from Mammy and Maeve, she still is and always will be, the only woman he has ever truly loved. Will she be ashamed when she hears about his dispensation from the priesthood? Will she understand? Poor Da had inadvertantly brought disgrace on the family by trying to spare them from the embarrassment of his debt, but Mammy's shame had been replaced with pride when her only son had become a priest – Father Damien. And now, he too is bringing shame on the family and the reneging of his vows will be the fodder for Ma Dooley and the village gossipers for months, probably years.

He tosses and turns until he hears the chirping of the dawn chorus in the chestnut tree and pale slivers of light are beginning to slip through the curtains. Soon doors will be opening and floorboards will be creaking, followed by the sound of water flushing and then the smell of coffee and toast drifting up the staircase. He buries his head in the pillow and finally drifts off to sleep.

Mary

She lets herself into the cottage and stands frozen in the hallway. Her face in the mirror is as white as a sheet and she feels icy cold. Her hands are trembling as she pours a glass of red wine and settles herself on the sofa with her feet curled up beneath her. She strokes Rufus absentmindedly, her thoughts preoccupied with the evening's events.

When she had seen Damien at Maeve's front door, she had thought she might faint. Still the same perfect specimen of manliness, a little older and more weathered perhaps, but still the same dear Dami. There was so much she'd wanted to say, things she could never say in front of Maeve and Fearghus, and she'd been relieved when the boys had eased the tension by chattering about school and soccer. Poor Maeve had tried valiantly to steer the conversation onto mundane subjects like the weather and the time had passed surprisingly quickly, although Mary had felt that time had ceased altogether. Was it wise to have agreed to see Damien tomorrow? Shouldn't she have just said goodbye and left it as it was? *No, Mary*, she thinks, *be brave. Tell him everythin' before he leaves, for you may never see him again.*

She's startled by the ringing of her cellphone. She fumbles in her bag and glances at the screen before answering it, hesitating as she regathers her thoughts.

'Hello, Niall!' Her voice sounds high-pitched and a bit hysterical.

'Mary, my love, are you alright?' he asks, 'you sound a bit agitated. Will you be joinin' me for a nice dinner tomorrow night? There's a new Thai restaurant in Patrick Street.'

'Oh, Niall, I'm so sorry . . . I can't,' she says breathlessly. 'I have a meetin' with an old friend. There's something I need to put to rest.' Rufus rubs himself against her leg, miaowing. 'Look, I need to feed Rufus right now but I'll see you Monday and explain everythin' then.'

She feels ashamed for being so abrupt with Niall but she just can't face confronting him right now, not until she's confessed everything to Father Damien. He's used to hearing confessions, anyway. 'Bless me, Father, for I have sinned . . .'

She puts Rufus' bowl on the kitchen floor and folds her arms around herself, gazing in a trance at the softly falling rain. The sky is darkening and the view outside has taken on the hue of a faded black and white photograph. *Dami,* she thinks, *dear Dami . . . just when I was startin' a new chapter in my book of life.*

She makes herself a cup of tea and climbs the staircase to her bedroom where she undresses hastily and pulls her nightshirt over her head, before going to the bathroom. She washes her face and peers into the mirror. Has she aged as graciously as Damien? She runs her fingers through her hair, exposing the faint signs of grey around her temples. *Damien's grey hair makes him look distinguished but mine just makes me look old,* she thinks, frowning, noticing the two furrows nestled between her eyebrows and the fine lines etched across her forehead. She sighs. *Ah, well, I am gettin' old. We all are. Twenty years is a long time.* She puckers her lips and the dimples appear. Those have been there forever. She dabs some night cream on her face, flicks the bathroom light switch and climbs into bed, trying to quell her jumbled, anxious thoughts.

She cradles the mug between her hands, staring across the room at the framed photographs on the dresser. *How true it is that a picture is worth a thousand words,* she thinks, ruefully, sipping her tea. *Well, all things must come to an end and great love will inevitably lead to great sorrow.*

She reaches for the book on her bedside table, opens it and reads the same words over and over again, unable to focus.

> *Someone I loved once gave me*
> *a box full of darkness.*
> *It took me years to understand*
> *that this, too, was a gift.* 17

Damien

He wakes abruptly from his short slumber and focuses on the day ahead. Supper with Mary. He feels nervous, apprehensive and fearful, as other emotions run wildly through his mind sumultaneously: anticipation, relief, sadness and, yes, shame.

The previous night, after Mary had left, he'd finally told Maeve and Fearghus that he'd abandoned the priesthood and was now just a teacher, looking for a job. They'd been shocked at first, unable to comprehend what he was telling them, questioning him over and over again. Finally, Maeve had said, 'You know I never wanted you to sacrifice yourself to the church, Dami. It was always Mammy's dream, not yours. Ah, but she was so proud o' you in your dog collar and robes; kept a picture of you on her dressin' table next to her bottle of *Anus Anus*. Little Damien and Brendan used to ask me why their uncle was wearin' a dress!'

'*Anus Anus!*' Damien had laughed, 'she kept that bottle displayed long after it was empty. You and Mary helped to drain it.'

'So we did,' said Maeve, smiling. 'But she did start usin' it again when she went to the Bingo with Frank. I can still recognise that smell anywhere. Mary was wearin' it . . . ' She'd stopped and looked at Damien anxiously, before changing the subject. She'd talked about the years they'd spent growing up without Da, just them and Mammy and Mary; how the girls had always felt that Damien was their protector, their defender, their anchor; how everyone had expected him and Mary to marry and that no one knew why she had settled for Seamus. 'There was talk that he abused her,' she said, frowning, 'hit her, punched her.   But she never told anyone, not even me. Sometimes I could tell that she had bruises on her face – that was when she'd wear make-up to try and cover the marks. And everyone knew that he was shaggin' that slag, Rosheen Murphy . . . and God knows how many others.'

'Feckin' snake!' muttered Fearghus, shaking his head, 'scum bastard.'

'We tried to find a decent fella for her after the divorce,' Maeve continued, 'but she just wasn't interested . . . not until Niall.'

'Niall?' asked Damien, looking confused.

'The new history teacher at the Convent. Fine fella. She brought him here for Christmas dinner.'

He'd felt a tightening in his chest, as though the air was being slowly forced out of his lungs. *She's in love with another man. After all these years, I'm too late.*

Maeve had chattered on but Damien was no longer listening. *What were you thinkin' anyway, man? That you could suddenly reappear in her life after twenty years and start again? You poor deluded fool,* he'd thought, scornfully. That was when he'd retired to his bedroom and had lain awake staring into the darkness, thinking about what might have been.

He lies still, staring at the ceiling which is reflecting the morning light. The silver paint around the light fitting is chipped and the pale silky threads of a cobweb are brushing against the bulb. On the wall in front of him hangs Mammy's picture, *The Waterlily Pond,* and to the right of it is another Monet print, *The Artist's Garden,* depicting rows of purple and pink irises blooming under a dappled light. He can almost see the garden, hear the bees and smell the scent of the lush carpet of flowers and he's reminded again of the garden they'd visited with Da. He used to love lying on Mammy's bed, studying the water lily painting when he was a boy. He'd borrowed a book about Monet from the library, hoping to better understand the artist's work, only to discover that Monet had said that 'everyone pretends to understand my art, when it is simply necessary to love'.

Simply necessary to love. What good can possibly come from rehashin' old memories and unfulfilled expectations with Mary? She has a new life now, a chance of happiness with Niall. Let bygones be bygones. The anticipation he'd felt on waking has now been replaced by a feeling of utter hopelessness and he resolves to cancel his meeting with Mary.

He climbs reluctantly out of bed and pads quietly to the bathroom.

Maeve

Maeve lies still, listening to the relaxing splashing sound of the shower, followed by the gurgling of the drain. She must remind Fearghus to sort out the drain or she'll call the plumber herself. He's procrastinating as usual. She glances at the bedside clock. Damien is up early. She turns over and pulls the bedclothes up to her chin. *Give him some space*, she thinks, *let him have some time alone.*

Fearghus is still snoring softly beside her and she tries to go back to sleep but the sound of his sonorous, shallow breathing, followed by a snort every few seconds, prevents her from drifting off and she's wide awake now. For a while she lies quietly beside him, watching his chest rise and fall with every breath and the collar of his pyjama top rise toward his ear and then subside as he breathes out. His head is thrown back, his mouth is open and the hairs of his ginger beard are messy and unkempt. She turns over impatiently and faces the wall. Her thoughts turn to last night's conversation. *He's not Father Damien anymore*, she thinks, still stunned. *He's left the priesthood . . . it would have broken Mammy's heart, but not mine. He's a brave man, to be sure.*

She'd noticed the look on his face when she'd mentioned Niall and how he had tuned out and stopped listening. *He's still in love with Mary. After all these years, he's still in love with her.*

She hears the back door close. *Where's he goin'*
so early in the mornin'? The village is still
asleep. I'll bet he's goin' down to the oak tree, to
our secret place . . .

She'll never forget the day when she and
Mary had made their way there one sunny
afternoon after lectures. They'd brought a bottle
of wine and some bread and cheese from Mr
Patel's and had planned to lie under the huge,
gnarled, shady branches and talk about so many
things. Things that were troubling Mary and
things about Fearghus that irritated Maeve.
They'd struggled with their bags as they'd
climbed over the fence, trying to avoid the nettle
patches, and Maeve had caught her new skirt on
a loose piece of wire. As they'd approached the
oak tree, they could hear a female voice giggling
and a deeper male voice whispering. Abandoned
on the grass was a black lacy bra and a pair of
black satin knickers and, as they got closer, they
could see two fat white legs, spreadeagled, and a
white freckly bottom heaving above them.
Maeve had let out a gasp and her hand had
sprung to her face.

'It's Seamus and Rosheen!' she'd cried, 'Oh,
God, Mary, it's Seamus!'

Mary's face had turned ghostly white and
she'd pressed her lips tightly together, but she
didn't utter a sound. She had spun around and
started running towards the fence, twigs snapping
under her shoes as she ran, with Maeve trying to
keep up with her. In the background they could

150

hear Rosheen's shrill voice. 'Jesus, Mary and Joseph, Seamus! Tis dose little feckers, Mary and Maeve!' When they'd emerged from the bushes, gasping for air, Mary's face had been set like flint. She'd refused to talk about what they had witnessed, other than to say that she was divorcing Seamus and, within two days, Seamus had moved in with Rosheen.

A merciful release for Mary, to be sure, thinks Maeve, swinging her legs off the bed.

Fearghus snorts loudly and opens his eyes briefly, staring vacantly at Maeve, before he turns over and goes back to sleep.

Damien

Damien creeps quietly down to the kitchen and lets himself out the back door. The sun is beginning to rise but everywhere there is a silky sheen of dew, undisturbed and fragile, like a delicate lace tablecloth over the hedgerows and trees. The windows of the parked cars are white and heavy with dew and the grass is damp and moist, forming dark green footprints behind him as he makes his way to the stream.

The village is soundless and still in the early morning mist but, as he crosses the little bridge, the mist starts to clear and he emerges from a foggy dark cloud into the light. He stops and looks down at his reflection in the calm water before resuming his journey. He passes the fields where cows and sheep are already grazing and climbs over the fence, avoiding the nettle patches over which he used to carry Maeve and Mary. He pushes through the spikey ferns until he comes to the shady patch under the oak tree where he settles down, pressing his back against the furrowed bark and scaly ridges of the huge trunk. He sits staring at the water, watching it move silently over moss-covered slabs of rock, forming small puddles. He knows every inch of this stream, the twists and turns and the deep rocky pools. This was where they'd taken the dare and jumped into the freezing water: that unforgettable moment when he'd first seen Mary as a woman and had vowed that he would marry her one day. The irregular bulge of the burl on the tree trunk with its swirling grain pattern and circular flat crust of bark, covered in yellow lichen, hasn't changed in twenty years. In fact, nothing in this landscape has changed and yet everything has changed.

You fool, he thinks, angrily. *You let her go. You weren't there to protect her from that bastard, Seamus.* The thought of Mary being abused and her soft white skin discoloured with purple bruises brings tears to his eyes. He sits, lost in thought, as memories of the times they'd sat in this very spot under the tree come flooding back. He pictures them laughing about Miss O'Leary saying *poo-etry,* or mimicing Father Farwell wiping his spectacles and Sister Evangelina showing the girls how to stick out their tongues for Communion. He remembers their conversations about Frank and Mammy and the improbability of them ever marrying each other and how they'd wondered where they'd be in five years' time. None of them had ever imagined that Damien would become a priest, like Father Farwell.

A former priest, he corrects himself.

He wipes away the tears that are now blurring his eyes and angrily flicks a stone across the stream, watching it skip over the surface, making ripples as it skims across the water. He used to ponder over Hemingway's poem about empty spaces in your heart, and the possibility that the people who once filled those spaces were meant to be relinquished to enable other people to fill the empty spaces. Perhaps the spaces were empty until the right people came along to fill them? Well, the spaces in his heart still contain the ghosts of Da and Mammy and Maeve and Mary and no one else could ever fill them. Anyway, he could never relinquish them – even if Mary is in love with another man.

He leans back against the hard fissured bark of the tree trunk and wraps his arms around his bent knees, resting his head on them as he stares at the soft green, feathery mat of moss under his feet. The earth is thick with the coppery-red leaves that Mary had always loved, now soft and damp from the morning dew.

Why did he come back? There are other places he can go, places where no one knows Damien Donnelly, former priest. He could get a job at a boys school and hide himself among the other anonymous, disillusioned members of the human race, all trying to escape those feelings that creep up like uninvited guests and make themselves at home.

He sits for an hour, his thoughts jumbled and confused until, drained and exhausted from lack of sleep, he heaves himself up, dusts himself down and starts to make his way back to his sister and Fearghus.

Mary

Mary sleeps fitfully, tossing and turning, until she finally gives up and throws off the duvet, leaving Rufus looking disgruntled. She swings her legs over the bedside and wriggles her feet into her slippers, then reaches for her bathrobe and pads downstairs. She lets Rufus out and takes the newspaper and bottle of milk from the doorstep. A passing dog walker waves and the dog strains on its leash, desperate to pounce on Rufus who stands his ground, looking blankly inscrutable. A jogger nods a greeting, calling out, 'hows it goin' there?' as he passes. Mary waits for Rufus to finish his roaming before she goes inside to boil the kettle and pop a slice of bread into the toaster. She'll make a nice pot of thick vegetable soup and some soda bread for supper tonight to keep her busy and ward off those unwanted thoughts that are invading her mind.

How is she going to explain to Damien what happened all those years ago? Will she be brave enough to tell him how bitterly she regrets the past and how much she has missed him and longed for him for over twenty years? Probably not. Will he be able to forgive her for conceiving a child out of wedlock and for divorcing her husband? Since she booted Seamus out she's felt as though, like Rufus with the furry white M on his forehead, she bears a big scarlet *D* on hers, proclaiming *Divorcee!* to the scandalised village, bringing shame and disgrace upon herself and poor dead Daddy. But she has to admit that since

Niall entered her life and, with Lola's wise counsel, she's started to feel as though she is worth something; not much, to be sure, but something. She's embarked on a new path and nothing is going to waylay her.

'You've always loved me, haven't you, Rufie?' she whispers, scooping him up in her arms. 'Pure, unconditional love. And I love you too, you beautiful ginger boy.'

She busies herself with preparing the vegetables and rolling the dough which she fashions into a loaf. She tidies the kitchen first and then the sitting room, plumping the cushions and polishing the antique rosewood dresser until, finally, as the evening begins to settle in, she pours herself a glass of wine and runs a hot bath.

She lies back, immersing herself in the mountain of bubbles, relishing the comforting feeling of the warm water enveloping her. She takes a sip of wine, savouring its velvety texture and the hint of herbs and . . . is it blackberries? She'd know that taste anywhere. *Blackers.* She smiles, picturing the three of them with their blackened lips under the oak tree. The overhead light is reflecting a burgundy glint on the rim of her glass as she takes another sip, feeling its comforting warmth rise up from her belly.

'It's time,' she murmurs, '*you do not have to walk on your knees for a hundred miles through the desert, repentin'* . . . '[18]

What would Daddy have said about her divorcing Seamus? Would he have been ashamed of his only child making a mess of her life? She knew that he'd never liked Seamus and had been left flummaxed when she'd married him. 'Mary, my love,' he'd said, frowning, 'are you sure yer makin' the right choice? You don't have to rush it, lass. You're young and beautiful, you have a good career ahead of you . . . ' But then he'd got sick and all their energy had been spent on trying to make him better.

Sometimes she wishes that she had moved away from the village, far from the whispering and the gossiping; gone to Dublin, where no one knew Mary O'Mara; done a 'geographical', as active alcoholics call it. But she knows that she would never have been able to escape from herself. What if she had never gone to Bridget's party and had waited for Damien to finish his studies? Would he have married her and not the church?

Ah, well, what's done is done. You can't undo the past. He's married to one greater than me now, she thinks, stepping out of the bath and draping herself in a thick towel.

157

Maeve

Maeve hears the back door slam and appears at the kitchen door in her bathrobe. 'You've been down by the tree?'

'Been cleanin' my head,' Damien replies, removing his jacket.

She can see that her brother has been crying and puts her arms around him. 'Oh, Dami,' she sighs, 'I'm so sorry that I didn't warn you that Mary was still here. I'm sorry for all the pain you've suffered: you, who deserve nothin' but happiness. But it's not too late, Dami. Go to her. Tell her that you love her, tell her that yer not a priest anymore . . . it's not too late. The good Lord knows you were meant to be together.'

'Maeve,' he says, shaking his head, 'dear Maeve. It *is* too late now. I left her with that scumbag, Seamus, and now she has her fella, Niall. God forbid that I should cause her more heartache. She's already suffered enough; leave her in peace now to find whatever happiness is left to her.'

Maeve's face flushes with frustration. Emotion bubbles up and floods across her face and her eyes flash angrily. 'What will you do, then, Damien? Suffer yer punishment for divorcin' the church? Hang yer head in shame? Why does everyone else but you deserve happiness? Always tellin' everyone how much God loves them . . . when will you realise that God loves you too? That He wants *you* to be happy?' Her voice is getting louder and she slams her fist on the table. 'Please, Dami, I'm beggin' you. Go to her and tell her how you feel. Tell her the truth.'

A bleary-eyed Fearghus appears in the doorway, his ginger hair in disarray. 'What's goin' on in here?' he asks, sleepily.

Maeve shakes her head in frustration. 'I'll go wet the tea. You fellas go sit in the dinin' room; I'll make us some breakfast. Talk some sense into this brother of mine, Fearghus.' She slams the kitchen door, muttering to herself.

Fearghus and Damien sit at the table in silence. The sounds of cupboard doors banging, cutlery clattering, cups and saucers clinking, water blasting out of the tap and the kettle lid being slammed emanates from the kitchen. The smell of burning toast wafts under the door as Maeve cusses loudly.

'Will you be watchin' yer mouth now, Maeve!' shouts Fearghus, 'effin' and blindin' in there!' He turns to Damien and shakes his head. 'Havin' her monthlies.'

She slams the tea and toast onto the table before returning to the kitchen, where she starts to unload the tumble drier, pulling out garments and folding them angrily. She grabs a pair of her large, practical cotton kickers and frowns, pursing her lips. Poor Fearghus – he's never seen her in black lacy knickers like Rosheen Murphy's. What do they say about an Irish husband? A man who hasn't had sex with his wife for twenty years and will kill any man who does. Perhaps she should shock him and buy a pair of black lacy knickers and see if she can excite him, like Rosheen used to excite all the fellas? She shakes her head. *He wouldn't even notice if I sat down naked next to him.*

For a moment she wonders if other wives wear big cotton knickers like hers? Mammy surely did. And Sister Evangelina. Maeve and Mary had once seen the nuns' laundry hanging in the Convent's back yard when they'd taken a short cut to the chapel – huge greying undershirts, nightshirts and enormous white cotton knickers. But no bras. They'd giggled and run away guiltily, afraid of being caught by one of the nuns.

She'll never forget kneeling behind Rosheen in the Convent chapel and being mesmerised by the movement in her teased beehive. As she stared at the magnificent lacquered dome she could see tiny insects burrowing in and out of it, like little black ants building a nest. Sister Evangelina had sent them all home and Mammy had spent hours with the nit comb, drowning the insects in a saucer of water, before washing Maeve and Mary's hair with a foul-smelling shampoo from Mr Patel's. Damien had been sent to the barber in Patrick Street and Paddy O'Sullivan had cut off his thick dark hair with his clippers. He'd looked different without his hair but Maeve still thought he was the most handsome boy she'd ever seen. He never seemed to notice that the girls were swooning at his feet; he only ever had eyes for Mary O'Mara.

He needs another visit to Paddy, she thinks. *And some new clothes. And we'll be chuckin' out those sellotaped specs of his; make him presentable again.*

She loads the clean folded washing into a basket and joins her men at the table.

'How'aya now, Maeve?' asks Damien, gently taking her hand.

She looks up sheepishly and smiles. 'Ah, sure you know yerself, Dami, I'm grand. Just grand.'

Mary

She takes the loaf of bread from the oven and places it on the windowsill to cool. The aroma permeates the little kitchen and she smiles, remembering how Damien used to re-enact a television advert whenever they stepped into Mammy's kitchen after school. He'd lift his head and sniff the air and recite, in a posh British accent, 'nothing says home like freshly-baked bread.'

'Ah, g'way wi'you!' Mammy would laugh, flicking him with a dishcloth. 'Go wash yer hands. I'll be wettin' the tea.'

Mary is starting to feel nervous and keeps glancing anxiously at the clock. Her hands are trembling as she tucks a few strands of hair behind her ears and takes one last look at herself in the hall mirror. She's wearing a pair of black jeans with a black sweater and the long, double-strand pearl necklace that had once been Ma's. Her hair is tied up with a red ribbon and her lips are stained a matching cherry red.

The doorbell rings and she inhales deeply before she opens it. Damien's large body is outlined in the doorframe and the porch light is shining above him, giving the appearance of a halo around his head. He hugs her gently, unsure of how she might respond, and proffers a bottle of wine before stepping into the hallway. He looks around at the once familiar interior.

The rosewood dresser is still standing proudly under the gilt-framed mirror and, in front of the bay window, is the worn old oak table where they used to play card games like *Donkey* and *Rummy*. Poor Seamus would always end up being 'Donkey' and would have to bray *eee-aww* three times. His face would turn scarlet as the other players pointed at him and laughed, shouting 'donkey!' 'Ah, just eff off, will ya?' he'd mumble, throwing his cards onto the table and pushing his chair back angrily. The four hard-wood chairs have been upholstered in a cream-and-green floral fabric and there's a vase of St Joseph's lilies on the table.

'Ah, Mary!' exclaims Damien, 'you've worked yer magic on this house. Frank would be so proud o' you.' He sniffs the aroma of the cooling bread and starts to recite in a booming voice, 'nothing says home like freshly-baked bread.' Mary shakes her head and laughs. The distinctive, trance-like music of Enya is playing softly in the background and the delicate notes float as light as a whisper.

'Glass o' wine?' she asks, hiding her shaking hands behind her back.

'Sure, that would be grand. Here, let me open it for you.'

They settle down on the sofa and Rufus immediately climbs onto Damien's lap, purring softly. There's a sudden awkward silence, until they both start speaking at the same time. They pause and laugh and the ice is broken. Damien starts talking again.

'D'ya remember when we were young and you said you'd like to be a ginger cat – with green eyes?' he asks, stroking Rufus.

Mary laughs. 'So I did. Just like Rufus. And, if I remember correctly, Maeve said she'd be a golden Labrador. She's always loved dogs, hasn't she?'

Damien nods and smiles and takes a sip of wine. 'I think I said I'd be an elephant.'

Mary chuckles. 'Well, we got pretty close, didn't we?' She reaches out to Rufus who is purring contentedly on Damien's lap and her fingers brush his. She jerks her hand away, embarrassed, her cheeks flushing, and looks down at the glass of wine in her other hand. She presses her lips together and runs her fingers nervously along the stem of the glass then turns to Damien. 'Tell me about Africa, Dami.'

He would much rather cup her perfect oval face in his hand and kiss those moist red lips but instead he starts to describe the wide open plains of savanna bushveld; the clear blue sky that stretches forever into the horizon; the harsh sun and the violent thunderstorms that end so suddenly, leaving the earth steaming and the grass glistening and shimmering.

He pauses and smiles, as the lilting notes of *Storms in Africa* waft simultaneously in the background. He takes another sip of wine and continues to describe the flora and fauna of

Africa, the unforgettable sight of giraffe and elephant, zebra and lion, and the peace and serenity of the bush, where time had seemed to stand still. His eyes light up as he tells Mary about the glorious gold and pink and orange sunsets, about the people who danced and sang, even during the toughest of times, and of their unfailing hospitality and warmth. He talks about the parish he had pastored with its eclectic mix of parishioners, like Malcolm in his beige car coat and Dorothy and Cynthia, so essentially British in the middle of that dusty little African town.

He pauses again, picturing the folk who had been a part of his life for so long, as images of Jerry and Dorothy and Cynthia flash before him. 'Once you've lived there, Mary,' he says softly, 'Africa is always with you.' He taps his forehead. 'It's here inside yer head.'

She sits, mesmerised, enthralled by the sight of Damien's strong muscled forearms, his large square hands with the jagged white scar across his finger, from the time he punched Seamus outside Mr Patel's, his neatly-cut nails and his clear golden skin which had always had a glow that made it appear to shimmer sometimes. Poor Maeve used to complain bitterly that Damien had inherited Da's darker skin tone, while she had Mammy's ruddy complexion. Da used to tell them stories about his maternal grandfather who was Spanish and Maeve would imagine herself as a flamenco dancer in a slinky, red, frilly dress holding a fan, her hair pinned into a chignon at the base of her neck. In her fantasy her hair was black and shiny, like Mary's, not reddish-gold like Mammy's, and her skin was the colour of milk chocolate.

Mary longs to reach out and touch the crinkles around Damien's intense grey eyes (he didn't have those crinkles when she last saw him), to run her fingers down his cheeks and along the lines on either side of his nose and into the corners of his mouth, to read his whole face with her fingers as though she were a blind person reading Braille. She already knows every inch of this face, anyway, and has pictured it clearly with her eyes closed for the past twenty years. She'd love to smoothe his silvery dark hair with her hand and rest her head against his chest, breathing the musky smell of young Damien's cologne, but she forces herself to refocus as he describes the places he has been. His deep lilting voice floats in the background and her mind drifts away to those halcyon days before Seamus robbed her of her future and Damien gave himself to the church.

He gets up to pour them both another glass of wine and they adjourn to the dining table. Mary serves the steaming soup from a porcelain tureen and cuts thick slices of warm bread, which they spread lavishly with butter. They eat in silence, their spoons clinking against the ceramic soup bowls, until Damien chews the last morsel of bread and drains his glass.

'That soup was grand, Mary,' he says, patting his stomach, 'and nothin' beats Mammy's soda bread.' He folds his napkin and leans forward, resting his arms on the table, looking into Mary's eyes. 'I've talked enough about me tonight, now tell me about you. Tell me about your life since we parted.'

She hesitates and looks down at her lap, fiddling with her napkin. Where should she begin?

'You knew about Daddy's illness?' she asks, looking up into his face. 'That was a terrible time . . . watching him suffer and being unable to help him.' She presses her lips together and looks away. 'He died here – in his bed . . .' Her voice trails off. 'I think I just buried myself in schoolwork after that.'

'I'm sorry I didn't get to see Frank before he died,' says Damien, frowning, 'he was a fine man. One of nature's true gentlemen. Helped Mammy a lot too.'

Mary nods and begins to recount her experiences as a teacher, her frustrations with girls who have no interest in poetry or literature and the predictable mundanity of her life before Niall. But still she makes no mention of him or Seamus. The mellowing effect of the wine relaxes them and eases the mood and they reminisce and laugh about Sister Evangelina and her dog, Angus, and mimic Father Farwell wiping his spectacles and Miss O'Leary saying *poo-etry*.

'You still love *poo-etry*, then Mary?' asks Damien.

She smiles. 'Oh, I do, Dami. You taught me to love *poo-etry*. I've still got that book of Yeats' poems that you gave me for my seventeenth birthday.'

'*Tread softly for you tread on my dreams . . .*' he quotes, smiling. 'I was a bit presumptuous, wasn't I?'

She looks away and when she turns back she has tears in her eyes. Damien studies her beautiful face with the the dimples on either side of her full red mouth. He yearns to touch her soft luminous skin and bury his fingers in her thick black hair, but too late now. He leans across the table and gently wipes away a tear that is quivering on her eyelid and threatening to trickle down her cheek. He holds it momentarily on his finger and licks off its saltiness.

They sit in silence, their eyes locked in an unspoken embrace, while the notes of *Only Time* float in the background. Still, no mention is made of Seamus or of Mary's betrayal.

'Maeve says you have a nice fella now. Niall?'

She flushes and looks away.

'He is nice. He's a good man. He . . . I . . .' She looks down and twists the napkin in her lap.

'Mary? What is it?' asks Damien, softly, 'you can tell me.'

She gets abruptly to her feet and tosses the napkin onto the table.

'Of course I can tell you!' she snaps, 'you're a priest. I know all about the seal of confession, Father Damien . . . people confessing their sins and their secrets and you have to listen and not tell anyone and just sit there in your robes and be impartial and detached . . .' She stifles a sob. 'Oh!' she cries, 'why can't you just be Dami . . . ?' Her voice becomes a whisper. 'Why can't you just be Dami?'

The colour has drained from his face. He pushes his chair back and gets to his feet and they leave the table without speaking. Mary blows her nose and wipes her eyes while Damien refills their wine glasses. They settle down on the sofa again with Rufus between them, licking his paws and wiping his face. Damien stretches his long legs and leans back, listening to the *bluk-bluk-bluk* sound of Rufus grooming himself with his sand-papery tongue. Finally, he speaks.

'It's time we talked about the past, Mary. We both need to find closure now. Why did you not wait for me?'

Damien and Mary

Slowly and haltingly she begins to tell him about the terrible night when Seamus had impregnated her in the coat cupboard at Bridget's house. About the unspeakable shock and horror she'd felt when she awoke and saw the blood on her knickers; the even worse shock when she had discovered that she was pregnant and would have to marry Seamus. And then, finally, God's punishment, killing her unborn baby, leaving her forever with the guilt and shame and the feeling of worthlessness.

'I have a big red *D* on my forehead now, Father Damien. *Divorcee*! I'm a scarlet woman, a sinner, condemned to eternal damnation . . .' Her voice trails off, 'and even you cannot pronounce absolution.' She turns and looks up at him defiantly, expecting to see pity and disgust but instead, she sees shock and rage and horror in Damien's pale, tortured face. His eyes are filled with tears.

'That scum bastard, Seamus!' he cries, 'oh God, Mary, I'm so sorry, I am so sorry. I vowed to protect you and I couldn't . . . I didn't. I failed you, Mary, I failed you.' He puts his head in his hands and Mary can see that they are shaking. She sits still, watching him silently, until he looks up at her and says, 'there's something I need to tell you now, Mary. I'm not a priest anymore. I've been granted dispensation; released from my vows.' He shakes his head and frowns. 'I was too imperfect to be a priest. I failed God and I failed you. I thought I could sacrifice myself on the altar of self-denial. But I failed.'

She jerks up suddenly, her hands reaching out to him.

'You? Failed?' she cries. 'Oh, God, Dami, you are the most humble, honest man I have ever known. Just like your da. No one could ever measure up to you.' She can't stop the tears that are coursing down her face, as she stares at him in disbelief. Her hand draws back to her open mouth. 'You're not a priest anymore? Did you say you're not a priest?'

He takes her hand and kisses the back of it, looking into her huge luminous eyes.

'Aye, I'm not a priest, Mary. I've been given dispensation. But this one thing I know to be true is that God is merciful and forgivin'. Oh, Mary, sweet Mary, it was Seamus' sin, not yours, that conceived your child. That bastard raped you, Mary. He raped you. He took from you what you did not give. God didn't punish you and take your child. He doesn't see a big red *D* on your forehead, Mary.'

She springs up from the sofa and turns away from him, stumbling towards the window. Her shoulders heave as she inhales huge gulps of air. Locks of hair are spilling down her long pale neck, into the little hollow that had always made her seem so vulnerable and never more so than now. Wee Mary O'Mara, whom he'd vowed to defend all her life, to save from life's cruel blows, and he failed her. He feels an overwhelming surge of love and empathy for this wounded, damaged, innocent child/woman and steps up quietly behind her. He puts out a hand and whispers her name. 'Mary.'

She turns and looks into his tormented face and throws herself, sobbing, into his arms. He pulls her against his chest, engulfing her, breathing in her sweet fragrance, murmuring in her ear.

'Oh, Mary, my sweet Mary Rose. There has not been a day since we parted that I did not think of you.'

His lips find hers and this time she doesn't turn away. She yields in total surrender to his urgent, passionate embrace and everything around her blurs as she feels herself unfolding into him. All the buried pain, the years of self-loathing, the condemnation and the hopelessness start to dissolve in the pool of this man's love and compassion.

Time stands still for Damien and he feels as though he's drowning, helpless in the whirlpool of his emotions and the acute arousal of his senses. Their two souls seem to blend into one as their tears mingle and they cling to one another, locked in a timeless embrace. He buries his face in her soft neck and breathes a deep, juddering sigh. *This is what I have denied to myself for all these years. Just to be a man in the arms of the woman I love.*

Damien

Dawn is breaking when he tears himself away from her. 'I don't want to leave you, Mary,' he whispers, 'I'm afraid that I'll lose you again and I could never bear the pain.'

'You'll never lose me again, Dami. Nothin' and no-one will ever come between us. T'was always meant to be.'

They'd been entwined together on the sofa for hours, not wanting to break the spell, both of them still unsure of what had transpired between them. All the years of longing and love denied had finally culminated in this magical reunion, when they'd been transported back to the time when they'd both known that they were destined to be together.

'It's the beginnin' of our lives today, Mary, the promise of fresh miracles, new dreams to dream, a new book to be written . . . ' He kisses her gently on her forehead, then cups her face in his hand. 'But, there's somethin' urgent I need to do, my love.' He heaves himself off the sofa. 'I'll catch you later. You get some rest now.'

He closes the door softly behind him and steps into the silent street, just as the golden light of dawn is creeping in, amber and rose-pink. The dew-drenched grass is glistening and the deserted streets and hedgerows are shimmering in an eery light, as the faint chirping of birds announces the beginning of a new day. Not a soul is stirring as he strides down the road with his hands deep in his pockets, contemplating a wondrous, splendid future, his heart bursting with inexpressable joy.

He quietly lets himself into Maeve's kitchen, removes his boots at the door and climbs the stairs softly, carefully avoiding the steps that creak. Then he lays himself down on the bed and slips into a deep, peaceful slumber.

Maeve

Maeve turns over and glances at the bedside clock – 5:00 am. Was that the kitchen door she just heard? She closes her eyes and drifts back to sleep, only waking again a few hours later.

The house is still silent, apart from the sound of Fearghus snoring like a high-pitched whistle. He'll be awake soon so she slips out of bed and creeps to the bathroom. She loves these private morning moments when she can make a cup of coffee and sit at the bay window downstairs, looking out at the unfolding day; watching the sky turn light, curtains opening, lights coming on, blinds going up in the tea room across the street, listening to the sounds of birdsong and the clanking of milk bottles.

I could have sworn that was the kitchen door I heard closin' early this mornin', she thinks. *Damien*? She puts her coffee mug on the table beside her and her gaze falls on the worn old book on the window ledge. She opens it and smiles. Mary Oliver, of course . . .

And now you'll be telling stories
of my coming back
and they won't be false, and they won't be true
but they'll be real. 19

'Would that be the aroma of fresh coffee I'm smellin'?'

Damien appears beside her, barefoot in his jeans, his hair tousled and with dark stubble on his face. He looks tired but elated, as though a great weight has been lifted from his soul. Maeve hands him her empty mug.

'It's brewin' in the kitchen.'

He returns with fresh coffee and pulls up a chair beside her.

'Been reading my *poo-etry* book?' he asks, smiling.

'Still Mary Oliver, I see,' says Maeve, closing the book, 'Mary's favourite too.' She sighs, gazing through the window. 'I do so love the early mornin's, watchin' the day begin . .' She turns to Damien. 'What time did you get in last night, Dami?'

He flushes and takes a sip of coffee. 'It was early this mornin' to be honest, Maeve.'

She looks at him expectantly. 'You were at Mary's til mornin'?'

'Aye, I was.'

'And . . . ?'

'And I did what you said. I told her, Maeve. And she loves me too. And we're goin' to be together now . . . '

'Ah, don't you be coddin' me, Dami! Oh, c'mere to me!' She flings her arms around him, laughing and crying, feeling the rough stubble of his beard against her cheek. 'Oh, glory be! At last! At last!'

'What's goin' on in here?' croaks Fearghus, appearing at the door in his pyjamas, rubbing his eyes. 'You'll be wakin' the lads, Maeve.'

'Damien and Mary!' cries Maeve, jumping up and down, 'Dami and Mary!'

'Ah, g'way outta here!' exclaims Fearghus, shaking his head, 'are you feckin' coddin' me?' He offers his hand to Damien and pulls him into a bear hug. 'Good on you, mate. Good on you.'

Maeve hurries to the kitchen and soon the smell of sizzling bacon fills the house. They sit around the dining table, tucking into eggs and bacon and toasted soda bread, while Damien shares the details of his and Mary's reunion. His face clouds over and his eyes flash with anger when he recounts what Seamus had done to Mary all those years ago, how he had destroyed her life and how she had blamed herself.

Maeve puts her hands to her face. 'Oh, that poor wee lass!' she cries, 'oh, my poor sweet Mary. Carryin' that burden all alone, thinkin' she deserved it! Oh God forgive me for not seein' it, for lettin' her suffer all alone.'

'That feckin' can o' piss!' shouts Fearghus, his face reddening, 'I'll smash his feckin' face in! Scum bastard!'

'No, Fearghus,' says Damien softly, 'I'll take care of it.'

They sit in silence, each lost in their own thoughts, until the door of Mammy's old cuckoo clock springs open and the cuckoo's song strikes the hour. Maeve looks through the window at the damp grey sky.

'Looks like it's goin' to be a soft day today. Will you be sharin' it with Mary, Dami?'

'I will . . . later,' says Damien, getting to his feet, 'but I'll be headin' into town first. There's somethin' I need to do.'

Maeve and Fearghus exchange anxious glances.

'Mind yourself now, Dami,' says Maeve, shaking her head, 'you take care, you hear me? You take care!'

Mary

Pale shafts of sunlight are filtering into Mary's bedroom when she wakes hours later. She snuggles under the duvet with Rufus curled up against her feet and watches the sun emerge and then fade and vanish behind thick, blueish-grey clouds. She lies still, listening to the gentle purring from under the bedclothes and her thoughts turn to the night before. Was it all real or just a wonderful dream?

She takes her mind back to the exact moment when Damien had arrived at the door, and relives every moment thereafter: the sight of him, the smell of him, the joy of having his presence beside her, listening to him recounting his life in Africa and watching the expressions on his face. That dear familiar face that she's never forgotten. She recalls the emotions she had felt of pure joy and love and fear: fear that he would reject her when she told him the truth and fear that he would be leaving her again for his God and her heart would not be able to bear it. She had seen the anger flash in his eyes when she'd told him about Seamus but, instead of condemnation, she'd felt his deep compassion and understanding. And then those profound, unbelievable words he had spoken: 'I am not a priest. I am no longer Father Damien.' At first she'd been unable to process what he was saying. How could he no longer be a priest? Wasn't that a lifetime vocation, a vow that could never be broken? Gradually, as she had begun to understand what he was saying, she had felt the faint stirring of a hope that had died so long ago and the possibility of a future with a different conclusion.

And, finally, that moment when he had been standing behind her and had spoken her name in a voice so charged with emotion, her heart had leapt in recognition. She'd found herself being engulfed by him, swept into the very essence of him and nothing had ever felt so right before. She feels a deep longing to see him again, to touch him and smell him, to reassure herself that it was all real.

She climbs out of bed and pulls on her robe, running her fingers through her tousled locks. The face staring back at her in the mirror looks the same, yet different – brighter, fresher, younger, as if a deep sadness has been erased from it. Damien hadn't been angry with her or disgusted when she'd revealed the horror of her dark secret and, for the first time since that terrible night, she'd finally been able to acknowledge that it was Seamus who had sinned against her and had stolen what did not belong to him. He was the perpetrator, not her.

But the greatest revelation of all is the realisation that she is forgiven, absolved from her disgrace and is not a scarlet woman. Oh, she knows that there will be shock and outrage and whispering in the village, especially at the Convent, and more so concerning Damien and the abandonment of his vocation. Ma Dooley will be in her element. Mary Rafferty's divorce had been the fodder for gossipmongers for months, just like Da's suicide had been years before, but Mammy had been redeemed when her son had become a priest. Father Damien.

How proud she'd been then, holding her head up high at Mass instead of looking furtively at the floor, sensing a new-found respect from Ma Dooley and her neighbours. What greater honour could there be, than to have raised a son who chose to deny himself and be married to the church?

And now he's returned as Damien Donnelly, former priest. Poor Mammy.

The ringing of her phone startles her and she glances at it before answering. Her hand flies to her face. 'Oh God!' she cries, 'Niall!'

Damien

Damien sets off purposefully towards town. He looks up anxiously at the ominous, leaden sky hovering over him like a grey blanket; the air is heavy with dampness and dark menacing clouds swirl angrily across the blackness. Traffic is moving steadily along the main road and mothers are hurriedly pushing infants in buggies, their collars turned up against the impending storm. The red number 10 bus rumbles by, its engine whining into a crescendo before winding down as it approaches the next stop, and a cyclist whizzes past him in a *whoosh* of air before he's gone.

He can still remember the names of the occupants of each house along the road – the Brennans, the Doolens, the O'Shaughnessys, the McNultys, the Foleys . . . They used to call Brendan Foley 'Monk' because he was so religious. *Nice lookin' fella, he was. Didn't he also become a priest?* Damien vaguely remembers a rumour that Brendan had committed a 'grave sin' with one of his parishioners. Ma Dooley would know all the details.

The colours of the brightly-painted houses are now muted and faded in the greyness of the day. *What will they be sayin' when they hear that I'm back?* he wonders. *That I've left the priesthood, that hallowed institution, and returned to my roots as plain old Damien Donnelly, Agnes*

Donnelly's lad? And worse, still, that I'm courtin' that shameful divorcee, Mary Rafferty?

He crosses the little bridge and stops briefly to gaze at the still, cold water below and the grassy verge leading to their secret place under the oak tree. He walks on towards Mr Patel's shop, with its colourful display of fresh fruit and vegetables on the pavement outside, and opens the door, inhaling the familiar pungent smell of incense and spices.

A much older and greyer Mr Patel is peering at a huge ledger in front of him, his murky spectacles balanced on the end of his nose. On the counter are big glass jars of bulls eyes, Cleeves toffees and pink and white marshmallows. He looks up and takes off his spectacles, squinting at the figure in front of him. His wrinkled brown face creases into folds of loose skin as a smile spreads across it. 'My god!' he cries, 'don't joke me! Is it yourself, Damien?' He turns to the back of the shop and shouts, 'Fatima! Fatima! Come see who's here!'

She appears behind him with a duster in her hand and shouts something in Hindi, rushing to greet Damien with her arms open wide. 'C'mere to me!' she cries, enveloping him in a hug. She smells of curry and of coconut and sesame hair oil. On a shelf behind her is the pot-bellied elephant god, Ganesha, that had terrified poor Maeve.

Mr Patel comes round from behind the counter and embraces Damien. 'Look at you there, son! So fine n'all. Skin brown like me!'

A surly-looking youth dressed in black, with his hood pulled over his head, enters the shop. 'Twenny Woodbine,' he says without looking up.

Mr Patel shakes his head. 'No tobacco sold here, lad. We are Hindus.'

The surly youth mutters something under his breath and slams the door of the shop. Damien turns, as if to go after him, but Mr Patel places his hand firmly on his shoulder.

'Leave it, son. They have no respect,' he says, shaking his head, 'no respect. My god, all of them from the estate. Like that Seamus Rafferty. Went bad when he start mixing with those scumbags. Well, you lie down with dogs, you're gonna rise with fleas. Ah, but you were always a good, respectful lad, Damien; never made no trouble.'

'Is Seamus still here?' asks Damien, trying to keep his voice steady.

'Still living on the estate,' replies Mr Patel, frowning, 'same house since you left. Still with Rosheen and the two daughters. Slags, like the mother. The oldest one have two babies already.' He shakes his head. 'My god, Damien, Rosheen the size of a house.' He spreads out his arms. 'Very sad, very sad. Your sister's lads good fellas, though; always nice and respectful, like you.'

'Ah, your ma, she would be so proud, Damien,' says Fatima, wiping Lord Ganesha absentmindedly with the duster, 'like when you become priest: Father Damien. How long you visiting, son?'

Damien hesitates. Should he tell them the truth and risk the news spreading around the village like wildfire or should he wait until a more appropriate time?

'A long time, I think,' he says. 'A long time.'

Mary

She swallows hard before answering her phone. Her throat feels tight and dry, as though there's an obstruction in it.

'Niall!' she says, her voice sounding quavery and breathless.

'I was missin' you, Mary,' he says. 'It's a grey day today. I thought maybe you'd fancy a visit to the pictures?'

She pauses and inhales deeply before replying.

'Niall, do you remember I said there was somethin' I had to put to rest? Remember the picture of my friend, Damien, Maeve's brother, the priest . . . the one who was in Africa? Well, it was with him. Only he's not a priest anymore and he's back . . . back here in Ireland.' She stops to catch her breath. 'He's stayin' with Maeve and Fearghus and . . . and I love him, Niall. I've always loved him but I thought I couldn't have him. I didn't want to tell you over the phone, I was goin' to tell you Monday.' Her voice fades into a whisper. 'I'm so sorry, Niall, I never meant to hurt you . . . '

Niall is silent and she can hear his angry, heavy breathing. Her hand is trembling and her mouth is dry. Seconds pass before he speaks.

'What the feck, Mary? What the feck? Are you coddin' me? You're in love with a priest?' His voice is getting louder and her heart is racing, as memories of Seamus and his temper resurface.

'I'm so sorry, Niall,' she whispers, 'I'm so sorry. I tried to forget him, I really did, but I couldn't, I just couldn't. And now he's back . . .'

'I always knew you were hidin' somethin', Mary. A feckin' priest! What next? Do you have no shame? Once a priest, always a priest. Yer gonna have a lot of explainin' to do, my girl. Well, good luck to you and your priest. I'll be seein' you, Mary.'

The line goes dead and she sits frozen, staring at the phone in her hand.

She doesn't blame Niall. How could he have known what she had been burying all those years, the truth that she had been denying to everyone but herself? She had tried so hard to convince herself that she could love Niall but it had all just been infatuation, fondness, romance. Not love. Love is what she feels for Damien. It always has done and it always will. What she feels for him is an emotion far deeper than affection, fondness, respect or lust. It's a fusion of souls, an incompleteness without him, a never-ending passion so pure and sacred, she cannot put it into words.

'I'm sorry, Niall,' she whispers to the phone in her hand, 'I'm so sorry.'

Maeve

Maeve and Fearghus are still sitting at the dining table when Damien leaves the house and sets off down the road. The joy they had both felt on hearing the news of Damien and Mary's reconciliation has been replaced by a fear of what he might be planning to do and where he is heading. Fearghus shakes his head. 'Seamus deserves everythin' that's comin' to him, Maeve. We should've known, we should've seen it. That poor wee lass, hidin' her pain all these years.' He thumps the table and the tea cups clink against their saucers.

Maeve wipes her eyes with her apron. 'It never made sense, her marryin' that tool. He never forgave Damien for punchin' his lights out for bullyin' little Ronnie Watson. Oh, what might Dami do to him now, Fearghus? What might Seamus do to Dami?' Her eyes are huge and full of fear. 'D'ya think you should be leggin' it down to the estate, love?'

Fearghus drains his tea cup and pushes the chair back noisily before heading upstairs to dress. Maeve sits quietly, staring into space, unsure of what to do next. Fearghus has always had a fiery, redhead temper and she has learnt to get out of the way when she sees that a storm is brewing inside him. But, underneath his tough exterior is a sensitive, caring soul who hates injustice – just like her brother. Now the two of them will be preparing to mete out justice to

Seamus to vindicate Mary's honour and Maeve is terrified. Perhaps Fearghus shouldn't go after all? She bites her lip, drumming her fingers on the table. Two hotheads in this house are enough without adding Damien to the mix.

Brendan, with his reckless, impulsive, fiery temperament is the son who inherited Fearghus' genes, right down to his red hair and freckles. Maeve frowns. How many times has he come home from school with cuts and grazes obtained from altercations outside the chipper? The school kids had stopped meeting outside Mr Patel's long ago after Damien gave Seamus 'a puck in the gob' as the boys called it. That was so out of character for Damien but he had always been on the side of the underdog, just like Da. But Da was never a proponent of violence and it bothers Maeve that Fearghus has always seemed quite proud of Brendan whenever he's come home looking dishevelled. 'Fair play, mate!' he'll say, ruffling his coppery hair. Young Damien, on the other hand, is uncannily like his uncle. Tall and dark and wise beyond his years.

Oh, please God let wisdom prevail now. Sure, we don't need another punch-up.

She grabs her phone and hurries up the stairs, just as Fearghus appears at the bedroom door, pulling on his jacket. 'Catch you later,' he mutters over his shoulder, as he hurries down the stairs, slamming the back door behind him.

'Oh, Fearghus, love!' calls Maeve, anxiously, leaning over the banister, 'don't you be doin' anythin' stupid now, please. Do you hear me, Fearghus?'

Damien

The air is heavy with dampness now and Damien feels as though he's suffocating in the humidity. Still, he presses on, the collar of his windcheater turned up and his hands deep in his pockets, as he strides towards the estate.

Surly-looking youths in black hoodies and baseball caps glare at him as he passes, fags pressed between their thumbs and forefingers. Girls as young as twelve, dressed in skirts so short he can see their knickers, their faces plastered in thick make-up, are flirting and giggling. Outside every dilapidated house is an old discarded mattress or a few broken chairs and bicycles with bent wheels. An old green Mazda with missing hub caps is parked on a verge and a thin mangy dog is sniffing in the gutter. Graffiti is plastered on some of the walls and in large black letters someone has scrawled, *Ireland belongs to the Irish.* In the midst of all the decay and despair and the weeds growing through the cracks in the pavement, a small white flower with a yellow centre is blooming between two slabs of cold, grey concrete.

Damien is approaching Seamus' house now – the house his widowed mother had lived in when he and Damien were friends. He can feel his heart racing as he approaches the sagging front door. A yellowing lace curtain flutters before his knock is answered and the door creaks open. Standing in the doorframe is an enormous, moon-

191

faced woman with purple hair, a fag in one hand and a pale baby on her hip.

'Whad'ya want?' she asks in a gravelly voice.

Behind her, Damien can hear a girl swearing and a child crying, then a male voice shouting, 'shut the feck up!' The smell of boiled cabbage wafts from the kitchen and he blanches. He puts out his hand. 'Rosheen?'

She peers at him from under her purple fringe.

'Jesus, Mary and Joseph! Is it yerself, Damien Donnelly?' She turns and barks over her shoulder, 'Seamus, c'mere. We have a visitor. Father Damien is at our door!'

A thin, emaciated man in grey track pants shuffles to the door. He looks confused as his bewildered gaze searches Damien's face. Then his lip curls and he sneers. 'Father Damien,' he says, spitting out the words contemptuously. His face is shrunken and sallow and a few of his teeth are missing. Little red thread veins criss-cross his cheeks and what is left of his greasy hair is hanging limply onto his shoulders.

Damien stares, shocked at the sight of the pathetic creature in front of him. A muscle twitches at the corner of his mouth and the vein running down his forehead pulses. His whole body is flexing with anger and his fist is clenching and unclenching in his pocket, as the deep rage that has been welling up inside him is about to erupt. They stand motionless, facing each other, while Rosheen hovers in the background, breathing heavily. Minutes pass until, suddenly, Seamus thrusts his hand into the band of his track pants and the silver glint of a cold steel knife blade flashes in front of him. At the same time Damien draws his clenched fist out of his pocket. His elbow jerks back and he prepares to punch Seamus in his ugly, drug-ravaged face, just as Seamus plunges the thin, sharp point of the knife blade towards Damien's neck.

Maeve

Maeve closes the door to her study. The rain that had been threatening earlier is bucketing down now. It would surely be foolish for Fearghus to follow Damien? She sits on the edge of her desk chair and frantically dialls Mary's number. The phone rings for several seconds before Mary answers it breathlessly.

'Maeve! I was about to take a bath . . . '

'Mary,' says Maeve, excitedly, 'Damien told us! We're just so happy for you both . . . just gobsmacked in fact, but Lord have mercy that we didn't see what was right before our eyes. Oh, you poor wee lass!'

'I couldn't bring myself to tell you, Maeve. The shame was just too great. I thought I was damned, unforgiveable . . . ' She pauses, 'and now he's back, and he loves me too . . . he loves me too, Maeve. We can start again.'

Maeve makes clucking noises down the phone.

'It was always meant to be, Mary. It was always meant to be. We all knew that.' She waits while Mary blows her nose and hesitates before she asks, 'and Niall?'

'Oh, Maeve!' cries Mary, 'I've broken his heart. God knows I never meant to . . . I wanted to love him, I tried to, but there was only ever room in my heart for Dami. He was so angry, Maeve. So angry. Like Seamus. I've never seen him like that.'

'Poor fella,' says Maeve, 'he was fallin' in love with you, Mary. I could see it in his face. You can't blame him for bein' angry . . . he's had his heart broken.' She stops and breathes deeply. 'But, it's Seamus we need to be talkin' about now. Dami has gone to the estate, Mary. He's lookin' for Seamus. Fearghus was goin' after him but it's lashin' out o' the heavens now. Oh, I'm so frightened for them both!'

'Oh, Maeve! God help them. What are we going to do? Shall we call the guards?'

Maeve pauses. Seamus won't be backing down when he sees Damien full of rage and retribution, ready to face his nemesis. Only the other day Ma Dooley told her that Seamus always carries a knife and has been involved in several stabbings and was recently under probation. He's also a drug user and is seldom sober. What might he do to Damien? She bites her lip, as she contemplates what action to take.

'Maeve,' says Mary anxiously, 'I think we should call the guards. Damien and Fearghus are no match for Seamus. He's got a knife, Maeve. He doesn't care. He'll kill them.' She starts to cry softly.

The back door flies opens with a bang and Maeve can hear the scraping of boots and the rustling of coats.

'Fearghus, is that you, love?' she calls.

Seamus

Damien unclenches his fist as the knife flashes in front of his face. Instinctively, he grabs Seamus' wrist and swings his head to one side at the same time, just as the blade slices past his neck and flies out of Seamus' hand, clattering onto the hard cement pavestone. He's about to launch his fist into Seamus' face, when his eyes lock with his tired yellow eyes and, for a brief moment, a glimmer of the old Seamus flashes before him. The freckle-faced boy he had befriended at the age of fifteen, after Da had died; the boy whose own father had died of liver disease, leaving a wife and six children to struggle on without an income – an alcoholic, abusive father, just like his son. *How much have I been forgiven?* he thinks. *There but for the grace of God.* He releases his hold on Seamus and slowly unclenches his fist, reaching his hand out instead. 'Seamus. It's time to forgive, time to fix the past.'

Seamus stands limply in the doorway like a deflated, wrinkled balloon. His dead eyes stare uncomprehendingly at Damien and tears start trickling down his face. He lifts his trembling hand and Damien reaches out and embraces him, feeling his bony protruding shoulders and breathing the stench of his foul breath and stale smoke. Seamus starts to sob, softly at first, until his whole body is shaking and he's gasping for air. Behind him, Rosheen is blubbering, her huge white body trembling, as the cigarette between her fingers burns down and the baby on her hip stares vacantly at the rain falling outside. Minutes pass, as she gawks in shock at the two men locked in an awkward embrace. Suddenly, she drops the burning cigarette butt and swears.

'Jesus, Mary and Joseph! What the feck? It's pissin' down outside! Would ya be comin' in now for God's sake before we all get soakin' wet?'

Seamus' body is crumpling like an empty paper bag as he hangs limply against Damien's chest. Finally, he straightens up and points to the front room where Rosheen is standing with the baby on her hip. Slouched on the torn shabby couch is a teenager with blue and pink hair, her eyes glued to the television. At her feet, on the sticky grey carpet, another young child is playing with a broken toy, while chewing on a breadcrust.

Damien follows Seamus to the kitchen and takes a seat at the orange, formica-topped table. They sit in silence, while Seamus lights up a Woodbine and blows smoke at the yellowing ceiling. The weak bulb in the overhanging light gives a pallid glow over the shabby, messy kitchen. Seamus looks down at the peeling linoleum floor and then at Damien. He shakes his head and gives a phlegmy cough before he begins to speak. 'I'm fucked, Father Damien,' he says, his voice almost a whisper, 'beyond redemption now. All the sins – I'm guilty.

Headed straight for hell, to be sure. Too late for absolution now.' He sucks on his cigarette and explodes into a rattling, raspy coughing fit.

Damien pushes a mug full of cold tea dregs and soggy cigarette butts aside and reaches out his hand. 'God love ya, Seamus. I'm not *Father* Damien anymore. I'm not a priest. Just a man like you. But we all get second chances, third, fourth, fifth chances. It's not too late, man, even for you. I can help you, Seamus. We can get you into rehab, clean you up, make your kids proud of you, break the cycle.'

Seamus looks up blankly at Damien.

'D'ya know what I did to Mary, Damien? D'ya know what a poxy, bleedin' scumbag I am? Not even yer God can help me now. D'ya remember Father Farwell tellin' us to choose the narrow road that leads to life, or we'll roast in hell for eternity? He tries to imitate Father Farwell's deep booming voice but his voice sounds frail and reedy. 'Small is the gate and narrow the road that leads to life, boys, but wide is the gate that leads to destruction . . . Well, I chose the wide gate, didn't I, and to be sure, I'll roast in hell now.' He pauses for a moment and looks puzzled. 'Did ya say yer not a priest now, Damien?'

'Aye, I did,' says Damien, 'I'm not a priest anymore, Seamus. I've left the priesthood . . . but I haven't left God.'

'Yer feckin' coddin' me? Well, we're both of us damned now.'

'No, Seamus,' says Damien, earnestly, gripping his thin arm, 'we're both of us forgiven, washed clean by the blood of Jesus. God can fix you if you'll let Him. He loves you, man.'

'The sacred blood of Jesus,' mutters Seamus, 'drippin' from his broken heart, like in Ma's feckin' picture. Those eyes were always followin' me, makin' me feel like it was me who had pierced his heart. . . . well, I did, didn't I?' He laughs a hollow, empty cackle.

A baby crawls into the kitchen, its hands and knees sliding along the cold, greasy linoleum floor. Seamus bends and gathers the child into his arms.

'Can Mary ever forgive me?' he asks hoarsely, 'I pierced her heart, to be sure.' He looks up into Damien's face. 'Can you ever forgive me for robbin' ya, Damien?' His chest heaves as he hawks a crackling, bubbling, wet cough.

'It's for Mary herself to answer that,' replies Damien, 'but, to be sure, I forgive you, Seamus. God knows, I've been forgiven much myself.'

Seamus' eyes fill with tears again and he bends his head to the infant on his lap. His stained, nicotined fingers are orange against the soft white baby flesh. '*Honour yer father and mother,*' he murmurs, shaking his head. 'Ah, we've both dishonoured our mammys in different ways, Damien. Thank God they're not here no more to see it. All the whisperin' and scandal. Seamus Rafferty, the feckin' addict loser, just

199

like his oul fella, and Damien Donnelly, the former priest. Ma Dooley will feed on it for years.' He slowly lifts his head and looks into Damien's eyes. 'Will ya go back to Mary now, Damien? Will ya tell her I'm sorry?'

Damien nods his head. 'I will, Seamus. Sure, I will.'

He gets up from the table and pats Seamus' bony bent shoulders before making his way to the front door, treading gingerly over the broken toys and half-eaten bread crusts. From the front room he can hear the strains of *The Jeremy Kyle Show* blaring from the television.

He lets himself out of the door into the thin drizzle. The sky is grey and misty and the road looks black and sticky, dotted with shallow puddles of glistening rain water. The same group of teenagers is now huddled under a bus shelter and the sweet, pungent smell of marijuana wafts around them. 'Hey, mista!' shouts one of them, 'got a few quid on ya?'

Damien shakes his head and strides on.

Damien

Maeve waits anxiously for an answer. She calls again from the top of the stairs. 'Is that you, Fearghus, love?'

'It's yer brother,' answers Damien from the hallway.

'Gotta go, Mary,' she says, breathlessly, 'he's home! Dami's home. I'll call you later.'

She rushes downstairs and casts her eyes anxiously over her brother, checking for bruises and blood. Satisfied that he's uninjured, she says, relieved, 'will you look at the state o' you, Dami! Soaked to your skin. Shall I be drawin' you a hot tub now? Then I'll be wettin' the tea. I think there's a lot you have to tell me.'

'Aye,' says Damien, removing his jacket, 'a lot.'

He slips gratefully into the hot tub and leans back with his long legs bent at the knees, letting the warm water lap over his head and shoulders and wash away all the filth and grime that seems to have penetrated beneath his skin. He closes his eyes and tries to unscramble the jumbled thoughts in his troubled mind. He had gone to Seamus' house with one intention only: to pulverise him with his fists, to make him suffer for all the pain he had caused Mary and Damien in the only language Seamus would understand. But, when he'd seen him standing behind Rosheen, hopeless and defeated, a pathetic, crumpled shadow of the old Seamus, Damien had felt a sudden surge of compassion for him. Images of Seamus' father had flashed before him – the town drunk, who'd brought nothing but shame and embarrassment on his family, who used to beat his wife and kids into submission. *That was all Seamus ever knew*, he thinks, *that was how a husband was supposed to treat his wife.*

After they'd become friends, Seamus used to tell Damien how his mammy would send him to the pub to try and persuade his da to come home or give him some money to buy food; he'd find him slumped over the bar, singing bawdy songs, with white foam frothing around his mouth. 'G'way outta here,' he'd slur at his starving young son. 'Away wi' ya to yer feckin' miser mammy; tight as a nun's knickers, she is. Sh'my money.' He'd smash his glass down on the counter and start singing, 'a mother's love is a blessin' no matter where you roam.' Seamus would return home empty-handed to a meal of bread and dripping, washed down with cabbage water, and his ma would have to go begging to the Vincent de Paul society.

Some nights his da would come home happy drunk, singing *Ireland's Call*. He'd sway with his hand over his heart, crooning, 'Ireland, Ireland, together standin' tall,' then he'd wipe his eyes before continuing, 'shoulder to shoulder, we'll answer Ireland's call.' *The feck you will,* Seamus would think, sneering at the sight of his dishevelled, red-eyed father. *Makin' a holy show o' yerself, you are, staggerin' around. Ya look a right moran, ya feckin' dosser.*

And then there were other nights when he'd come home angry drunk, swearing and kicking the door, lashing out at Seamus with his leather belt with the curved rim of the buckle that would gouge his flesh, and Seamus would have to barricade himself and his mammy in the bedroom with the wardrobe pushed up against the door.

Damien had nearly wept when Seamus told him how his da had promised him a bike for Christmas if Seamus gave him his earnings from his paper round. He'd promised to make up the price difference but, when Seamus had tearfully asked him on Christmas morning where his bike was, his da had said, 'what bike?' Mr O'Keeffe had once given Seamus two homing pigeons which he had planned to sell, but one day he had returned home from school to the rancid smell of boiled chicken and the discovery that his da had killed the birds and made a pigeon pie.

And then, one dark wet night when Seamus was thirteen, he'd found his father's lifeless body slumped over the bar counter after closing hour, his cheek flattened against the hard cold wood and his tongue lolling out, with blood-flecked foam frothing around his mouth. Little wonder then, that Seamus had always loved coming home with Damien to the smell of hot bread and mutton stew and Mammy clucking around them, ensuring they were warm and fed, insisting that they wear a jumper if they went outdoors. Little wonder too that Seamus had started drinking and drugging to escape his hopeless reality.

Damien lathers himself with Maeve's magnolia body wash, rinses it off and heaves himself out of the tub. He dries himself vigorously, frowning as he thinks of Seamus and his wasted life. *He looks as though he's on his last legs and that wheezin' cough needs urgent attention,* he thinks. *I'll seek Father Farwell's advice on Monday, see what we can do for the poor fella. I'll be needin' to see Father anyway and face his disappointment once and for all, see if I can arrange a few interviews, get the ball rollin' . . .'*

His thoughts turn to Mary and he feels a surge of excitement at the prospect of seeing her later. He smiles, picturing her sweet, lovely face.

Mary Rose O'Mara, you stole my heart away complete.

Father Farwell

Father Farwell is sitting behind the huge, carved, mahogany desk in his study, preparing his sermon for the evening mass. It's always difficult to limit himself to twenty minutes when there is much he has to say about the behaviour of his congregants, especially the young ones. Oh, yes, he's seen them smoking and drinking on street corners, the girls in their tiny skirts that all but cover their private parts; no modesty, no shame but, sure, tis the parents who are to blame – thinking they can come to Mass, seek absolution for the sins of the past week and go out and commit the same sins all over again. It's almost 'mission impossible', trying to get them into heaven. He pours himself a generous tot of whiskey and swallows a mouthful of the rich amber liquid.

On the desk in front of him is a file with **Damien Donnelly** written across it in bold black letters. Impressive CV, to be sure. He'd be an asset to the college but why, in God's name, would he have sought dispensation from his vows? He was always a good lad, took care of his dear ma and sister and wee Mary O'Mara after her mammy died; made his ma so proud when he entered the priesthood. Everyone thought he'd marry Mary O'Mara but, begorrah, she surprised us all, marrying Seamus Rafferty. Biggest mistake of her life. Ah, well, we all make mistakes and he's proud to be God's representative, pronouncing absolution to sinners in the Sacrament of Penance and Reconciliation. What greater honour could there be? He takes another sip of whiskey.

Whatever became of young Brendan Doolen? he wonders. *Good-looking lad, he was too.* He'd last seen Brendan after he was newly-ordained – young and bearded and handsome. He'd become parish priest at St Dominic's in Ballyclogh and had started a worship group there. He used to play the bass guitar, if he's not mistaken. The youngsters adored Father Brendan and the church numbers had grown under his pastorage. Then, *poof,* he had suddenly disappeared, just vanished into thin air. Rumours abounded at the time that he had been sleeping with a fellow band member. Ah, well, Ma Dooley would know all the details.

Father Farwell shakes his head and wipes his spectacles with a tissue from the box he keeps on his desk, holding them up to the light to check for any specks he might have missed. On the wall directly in front of him is a huge, gilt-framed painting of *The Sacred Heart of Jesus*, by Pompeo Batoni. A beautiful, pale-skinned, blue-eyed young man is holding a wounded, thorn-covered heart in his left hand and is pointing to it with his right hand in a two-fingered salute. He adjusts his spectacles with both hands and sighs. *Ah, well, to be sure, it's not easy to live the consecrated life and, as St Paul reminds us, it's better to marry than to be aflame with passion.*

Still, he thinks, proudly, *I wish that all men could be as I myself am.*

He turns to the bookcase behind him, searching for a suitable reference book. There are piles of manuscripts and books in disarray cluttering the messy bookcase and rosaries and crucifixes of various sizes on the top shelf. He turns back to the pad on his desk, takes another mouthful of whiskey and glances out of the latticed window. *Holy Mother of God! Was that Seamus Rafferty entering the side door of the church? Surely not. He hasn't set foot near the church in years. Ah, well, God help him, poor fella. Sure, there's hope for us all.*

He returns to his pad and starts making copious notes.

Mary

She glances anxiously at the clock. Thank God Damien is safely back at Maeve's and is apparently, uninjured. Perhaps he didn't go to Seamus' house, after all? She is aching with longing to see Damien again, just to have his presence in her home and to feel assured that he won't ever be leaving her again. She knows he'll come and she will wait.

She puffs up the cushions and straightens the blinds, glancing at her reflection in the mirror above the dresser. Is she imagining it, or is her face glowing? Her eyes seem to be brighter today, reflecting the deep blue of the top she's wearing. She frowns at the loose tendrils of hair that are cascading onto her shoulders and tries to gather them together in a knot at the nape of her pale slender neck. Rufus rubs himself against her leg, purring, and she lifts him up in her arms and kisses him. 'Ah, you're a beautiful boy, my Rufie,' she murmurs, carrying him to the kitchen.

The door bell rings and she catches her breath, smoothing her skirt as she goes to answer it. She opens the door to a beaming Damien, clutching a bunch of colourful wild flowers – bright pink dog roses, yellow mountain reed and purple sprigs of lavender. He hands them to her with a flourish and a bow and recites in his deep, rich voice:

To see the world in a grain of sand
and heaven in a wildflower,

hold infinity in the palm of your hand
and eternity in an hour. 21

Mary blushes and takes the flowers, clutching them to her chest, before placing them on the dresser. Then she turns to Damien who is standing before her with his arms outstretched and buries herself in his broad chest. He strokes her hair, releasing the shiny locks that tumble down her shoulders, cups her face in his hand and kisses her lips – softly at first, then more urgently. She melts into his embrace, feeling as though she's turning to liquid. When they separate at last, she looks up into his dark grey eyes and sighs.

'I used to think I was the happiest girl in the world when we were toastin' marshmallows at Mammy's fireplace,' she says, smiling, 'but, right now, I *know* that I am the happiest girl in the world. And, Dami . . . I do so love you.'

'Ah, Mary Rose,' he whispers, 'I have loved you since I was a lad and I will love you till I die. We have the rest of our days for love now and nothin' will ever separate us again.'

She takes him by the hand and leads him to the kitchen where she boils the kettle and prepares the tea. She fills a vase with water and arranges the flowers, releasing the sweet earthy fragrance of lavender. Damien watches her moving gracefully from one task to the next: reaching up to for two mugs on a shelf, bending down to retrieve some fallen leaves from the

209

floor, pouring milk into a jug, pushing her hair out of her face. Her ordinary, day-to-day household chores, of which he has never been a part, but which are so extraordinary to him now. She tugs at a drawer and frowns as it sticks. Damien smiles.

'That drawer has been stickin' since Frank was alive,' he says, getting to his feet. 'Here, let me help you. I can see you need a handyman, Mary Rose.'

She nods and sighs. 'I never wanted to bother Fearghus,' she says. 'Daddy wasn't much good at fixin' things . . . and then he got sick, so . . .' She shrugs.

Damien tugs at the drawer and the cutlery inside it rattles as it jerks open. He puts his arms around Mary. 'You don't have to worry now, Mary, my love, I'll take care of you. This house will be ship-shape before you know it.'

She looks up at him and smiles. 'You have no idea how happy that makes me, Dami. No idea.' She puts the tea pot on the table and opens a packet of digestive biscuits before pulling up a chair. 'Now, will you please tell me about your visit this mornin'?' Her face clouds over. 'You went to see Seamus, didn't you?'

They sit facing each other at the table, while Damien recounts his visit to the man who was once Mary's cruel, violent husband. He describes the filthy house, the enormous woman who came to the door and the pathetic, skeletal creature who used to be Seamus.

'He's a broken man, Mary, a remnant of himself. I went there to destroy him, to punish him for what he did to you, to us, but when I saw him standing there like the stuffing was gone out of him, I just felt pity. I remembered his oul fella and the humiliation he brought on his family: Paddy Rafferty, the town drunk. That's all Seamus ever knew.' He frowns and helps himself to a biscuit. 'He only knew violence, Mary, never knew love. And now, his debauched lifestyle has caught up with him.' He pauses and takes her hand. 'He asked for forgiveness – from me and from you. I have forgiven him. Now, you must choose. Can you ever find it in your heart to pardon him, to forgive him for trying to destroy your life?'

Mary's eyes fill with tears and she brushes them away impatiently. 'He did destroy my life, Dami,' she says angrily, 'you have no idea what he did to me.'

Images of Seamus' hate-filled red face flash in front of her and his stinging words, 'the best part o'ye ran down yer ma's leg', ring in her ears. How can she ever forgive him for taking away her future with the man she was supposed to marry? But then she looks into Damien's earnest face, with the deep lines etched from years of pain, and she sees the warmth radiating from his eyes. She takes his hand and kisses it. *Seamus didn't win*, she thinks, *we won, God won. He gave me back my love. He forgave me and He's forgiven Damien. Who am I not to forgive in turn?*

'Dami, I'll try, so I will. With God's help, I'll try.'

Father Farwell

Father Farwell looks up at the clock: time to prepare for the evening Mass. He closes the door of the rectory and makes his way to the sacristy, stopping to break off a stalk of lavender from the bush under the window. He crushes the indigo flowers between his fingers and inhales the soothing, earthy, floral scent which has always had such a calming effect on him. It reminds him of his dear departed *Mater*, bless her soul: those little pouches of dried lavender that she used to keep under her pillow or nestled amongst her lace handkerchiefs in one of the drawers of the tallboy.

The dark clouds that had been hovering ominously that morning have been displaced by soft, white, fluffy clouds like balls of cotton wool and the heady, seductive aroma of jasmine is floating in the air. As he enters the church, beams of late afternoon sunlight are streaming in through the high windows, reflecting off the gold crucifix above the altar. The intoxicating smell of St Joseph lilies permeates the air, overpowering the musty smell of old hymn books and mould.

He approaches the altar and, to his right, he can see the figure of a man draped over the altar rail. He hesitates and waits for the figure to rise but observes no movement. He comes closer and gasps, as he recognises the hollow face of Seamus Rafferty, ghostly-grey against the dark wooden altar railing. A single shard of pale sunlight is cutting across his face like a sword. His eyes are open, staring vacantly at the crucifix in front of him, and around his mouth is a brownish mass of foam. Father Farwell touches his shoulder gently but his body is stiff and cold, like the marble statue of St Jude (patron saint for the most desperate, hopeless and impossible cases), keeping watch over Seamus from the plinth behind him.

'Holy Mother of God!' he cries, recoiling, 'Lord, have mercy on his soul!'

For a moment he stands glued to the spot, unable to think or to act. Then he stumbles out of the church and hails a passing Garda van.

Seamus' thin ravaged body is carried out of the church on a gurny, minutes before the altar boys arrive for evening Mass.

Maeve

Maeve is preparing the stew for dinner – Damien's favourite, another of Mammy's recipes. Tonight he'll be accompanied by Mary and it will be just like it was in the old days when they were all together with Mammy and Da.

She sighs with contentment, remembering the three of them gathered around the fireside in winter, toasting marshmallows, or lying in their shorts under the oak tree in the dappled summer sunshine, reciting *poo-etry*. Always together. Who could ever have imagined that life would take such a dramatic turn? That instead of Mary marrying Damien, she'd been defrauded by Seamus Rafferty? Ah, well, to be sure, God works in mysterious ways. All that matters now is that Dami is home and he and Mary are together again. And don't all fairytales have happy endings?

She hums happily as she opens the pantry door and pulls out the vegetable rack. 'Oh, Janey-Mack!' she cries, 'we have no taytos. We won't be havin' a stew without spuds! Fearghus, my love,' she calls from the kitchen door, 'will you leg it to Mr Patel's for me? I need spuds for the stew.'

Fearghus sighs, as he puts down the newspaper and removes his slippers. He pulls on his jacket and boots and leaves quietly out of the back door, looking up hopefully at the pale sky.

A group of women are gathered outside Mr Patel's shop, babbling and wailing, some of them wiping their eyes with their aprons. As Fearghus enters the shop, Fatima Patel starts shrieking in her high-pitched voice, waving her hands wildly in the air.

'Oh, Mr Fearghus!' she cries, 'did you not hear the news? Seamus Rafferty is departed.'

'Departed?' asks Fearghus, looking confused, 'where's he gone?'

'Now, that is a good question,' says Mr Patel, quietly, 'he's deceased . . . passed away.'

Fearghus frowns. 'Deceased? Dead?'

'Dead as a dodo,' nods Mr Patel.

From the room above, Fearghus can hear the strains of a Bollywood movie and the thudding of feet on the wooden floor. Fatima starts wailing again and Mr Patel ushers her to the back of the shop. 'Be hush, now, Fatima,' he says, 'be hush.' He returns to Fearghus who is standing at the counter, frozen in shock, and proceeds to inform him in detail about the passing of Seamus. 'Priest find him resting in peace . . .'

Fearghus listens in astonishment and almost forgets to buy Maeve's potatoes, such is his haste to get home and share the news with the family. He runs until he's breathless and finally bursts into the kitchen.

'Will you look at the state o' you, Fearghus!' cries Maeve, as he collapses, panting, onto a kitchen chair, 'sure, you're too old to be runnin' now!'

216

'Seamus,' says Fearghus, gasping for air, 'Seamus. He's dead!'

'What are you talkin' about, Fearghus?' says Maeve, shaking her head, 'Damien saw him yesterday.'

'Father Farwell found him dead in the church, Maeve. Slumped over the railin'. Died just like his oul fella.'

Maeve's face turns pale with shock. She puts her hand over her mouth and her eyes get bigger and bigger, as Fearghus recounts the details of Seamus' demise.

'God have mercy on his soul,' she whispers, 'we'll have to tell Mary and Damien.'

Mary and Damien

Mary hums as she removes the bread from the oven, ready to take to Maeve's. She looks through the open window at Damien who is busy re-erecting the washing line which had blown over in the storm. Today has been a fine day, with the sun peeping through the woolly clouds, the streets washed sparkling clean after the rain and, best of all, Damien being a part of her day-to-day life. She watches him bending and pulling the wires taut, the muscles of his forearms tensing and his greying hair flopping over his brow, and she feels a surge of affection for him.

For years she had convinced herself that she was happy, or if not happy, content. Content with filling the week days with schoolwork, watching television in the evenings and visiting Maeve at the weekends. It was as though she'd been living in a box with windows but no doors. She could see the landscape outside but she couldn't get out and no one could get in. It was safer that way, a manageable world. She was grateful for her cottage and her job and for the unconditional love of her faithful companion, Rufus, but sometimes she'd felt an overwhelming sense of loneliness. Like the times when she wished she could visit the botanical garden again or walk on the promenade, eating ice cream, or go to the pictures – all activities she would imagine doing with a male companion. When Bridget O'Hara had described her weekend visit to the beach and her walk along the promenade with her fiance, Mary had suddenly wanted to cry. She'd felt helpless and unqualified to change a light bulb that was too high for her to reach or to fix the swollen drawer and a dripping tap, or to change the wheel of her bicycle, although she knew that Fearghus would help her, and he often had. 'All you have to do is ask, Mary,' he'd said, but she was loathe to become a tiresome, feeble parasite, encroaching on his family time.

She was always cheerful and friendly at school but when she was alone at home with Rufus, she would often cry and surrender to the sadness that would glide over her smoothly and effortlessly, like a shadow, until she was engulfed by it. Some nights or weekends, especially when Maeve and Fearghus were away and she'd a few glasses of wine, she'd look at old photographs and end up curled in a foetal position on the carpet, crying until her eyes were red and swollen and she had no more tears left to cry. Afterwards, she'd put blocks of ice on her eyes until the swelling subsided and apply eyedrops to erase the redness. She'd go back to school the next day smiling, as though nothing untoward had happened, but her eyes would have a peculiar iridescent shimmer, a strange sparkling clarity and brilliance, like aquamarine gemstones.

And then, out of the blue, Niall had entered her life. She'd been unprepared and taken by surprise that he should want a relationship with her and she'd been guarded for weeks, afraid of stepping out of her box. But he had systematically bashed down the walls and forced her to take small tentative steps beyond its confines and then, just as she was emerging from the hard protective shell of her crysalis and finding her wings at last, Damien had reappeared.

Watching him now, working in the garden, filling the bird feeder with seed, watering the pot plants, just having him here in her home, has never felt so right and she feels full of gratitude and love. She's startled by the ringing of her phone and glances quickly at the screen before answering it.

'Hello, my love,' she says, smiling.

'Mary,' says Maeve, breathlessly, 'sit down, darlin', I have somethin' to tell you . . . Seamus is dead!'

'Seamus? Dead?' cries Mary, lowering herself slowly onto a chair.

Through the open kitchen door, Damien can hear her raised voice and looks up to see her seated at the table with her hand to her mouth. He hurries to the kitchen and listens to her astonishing conversation with his sister. Finally, Mary drops her phone onto the table and looks up at Damien with wide eyes. 'He's dead, Dami. Seamus . . . he's dead. Father Farwell found him dead at the altar.' She shrugs and presses her lips together. 'I guess his body just gave up.'

Damien seats himself at the table and runs his fingers absent-mindedly along the woodgrain and over the indentation where someone, years ago, had left a hot iron. He and Mary sit in silence, processing the news they've just heard. The ticking of the clock, the roar of the Number 10 bus and the slight tremour of the dresser in the sitting room punctuates the silence. He frowns. 'He must've gone to the church to seek absolution, to make his peace with God. Sure, he was lookin' wasted, but . . .' He shakes his head. 'I guess his poor body was finished . . . just gave up like his oul fella's. A blessin' really. Poor damaged soul; just like his da.' He shakes his head and says, softly, 'wounded parents raise wounded children.'

Mary takes his hand. 'You did good, Dami. You did what was right. You made your peace with him and now I must do the same . . . leave the past behind and start the future.'

She smiles. 'Does that mean I'm a widow now?'

221

Damien

He pushes the creaky old iron gate which leads to the walled garden of the rectory and steps into a riot of colours – poppies, cornflowers, evening primrose and the cheerful yellow heads of dandelions poking their way through them all. He's looking forward to getting his hands dirty again in Mary's little garden, to feel the rich brown earth between his fingers and smell the soil after the rain.

He seats himself on the wood and iron bench facing the charming old manse which is draped with virginia creeper in shades of copper and burnished gold, blended into patches of bright green. Against the fence there are neatly-tied climbing roses forming a tapestry of pale yellow blooms, and the sweet smell of jasmine and roses hovers in the air. The sash windows of Father Farwell's study are open and strains of Beethoven's *Fourth Symphony* are wafting into the garden. Damien watches an exquisite cerise pink and black butterfly settle on a geranium, then closes his eyes and lifts his face up to the sun.

His thoughts turn to the times when he used to sit in the old Parker Knoll chair on his little verandah in the baking sun, looking out at his withering garden, listening to Beethoven, feeling lonely and depressed. He can still recall the unmistakeable smell of the melting red *Cobra* floor polish. He could never have imagined then, that one day, this day, he would be sitting in the rectory garden, contemplating a very different future. So much has transpired since his departure from Africa and his arrival in the motherland, he can scarce process it all: his joyous reunion with Mary, his meeting with Seamus, and now his sudden death. And yesterday he had received a letter from Cynthia, regaling him with details about his ex-parishioners and his replacement, Father Innocent Khumalo . . .

I hate to have to tell you that your lovely garden is now just a yard, planted with mealies . . . Dorothy and Malcolm have been seeing one another and seem very happy together. Dorothy has actually lost a bit of weight and Malcolm has come out of his shell, so they've been a blessing to one another.

Jerry has been leading the walking group, but it's not quite the same as when you were here. Sometimes it's just too hot to venture out, anyway.

I can't quite believe it, but I have a grandchild on the way – my dear Emma is pregnant! So, that is something to look forward to.

Life continues to be challenging here, what with water shortages, power outages and certain foods in short supply. The dams have almost dried up now, due to the severe drought and I'm so thankful for the borehole and generator. As you can imagine, the bush is sparse and brown – unlike the green fields of your homeland. I often picture you striding in the countryside in the gentle mist – sounds blissful to me!

Anyway, we soldier on and try to focus on the positives. We do miss you enormously but I hope that you are happy and fulfilled and have found the peace that you so deserve. Perhaps one day you'll be abe to share the truth with me?

Images flash before him of the folk he once pastored in the town he once called home. He remembers them all with great fondness. Guileless, unsophisticated Jerry, with his passion for the bush; vulnerable, sensitive, anxious Dorothy; sad, beige Malcolm. And sunny, cheerful, lovely Cynthia with her green eyes and golden hair. Like these dandelions, pushing through her challenges and problems, thriving in difficult conditions, bearing her trials with such grace and dignity. Cynthia MacDonald. She will always hold a special place in his heart. *She'll be a wonderful grandmother,* he thinks, *a natural.* It pleases him to know that she and Dorothy are happy and that they both have something to look forward to, just as he does.

A hairy bumblebee hovers over the yellow primroses and he watches its short stubby wings flying back and forth, defying the laws of aerodynamics. He remembers Jerry telling him that, technically, a bumblebee should not be able to fly because of its heavy body and short wings, but that it doesn't flap its wings up and down like honey bees do. 'A bumblebee in your garden is a sign of a healthy garden,' he'd said earnestly. Damien can't remember ever seeing a bumblebee in his garden at the vicarage. *Ah, well, there's a lesson to be learned from the bumblebee,* he thinks: *no one told it that it shouldn't be able to fly.*

Cynthia had given him a book called *The Meaning of Flowers* for his last birthday and he'd been fascinated to learn that the pitiful, humble dandelion with its thin petals and jagged leaves represented happiness, simple joys, good companions and 'the presence of the inner child who often forgets to play'. If his memory doesn't fail him, the flower had been described as a gift to a loved one, promising total faithfulness. Chastity. The only time his vow of celibacy had ever been tested during his tenure as a priest was during his relationship with Cynthia, when he realised he was just a man. He can still recall Malcolm's soft voice: 'It is behoven in the scriptures for us all to be chaste, to be pure and virtuous.' *Well, I passed that test,* he thinks, idly, watching the bee hover over the flowers. *And all the while this little bumblebee keeps the cycle of life turning.*

The beautiful, melodic notes of *Fur Elise* are now floating across the garden and Damien heaves himself up and makes his way to the rectory.

Maeve

Maeve adds the last few slices of potato to her stew before washing her hands and wiping them on her apron. She glances up at the clock. She must get ready before Maeve and Damien arrive. She calls into the boys' bedroom. 'Don't you be goin' out on the razzle tonight, lads, gettin' rubbered!'

'Sure, we will, yeah!' shouts Brendan, 'we're goin' for a swell.'

'Ah, the cheek o'you!' laughs Maeve, as she gathers up the two wet towels on the bathroom floor and flushes the toilet. 'And don't forget that we have a guest in this house now!'

She peeps into Damien's bedroom. The bed is made, his clothes are folded neatly on the chair, everything is ship-shape – it's as though no one is actually living in there. She feels a surge of compassion for her humble, unpretentious brother who sacrificed so much for the family after Da had left them. She'd always known that he'd wrestled with his own demons of depression and sadness and she'd been concerned about him when they'd visited him in Africa. After she and Fearghus had retired to bed in the evenings, drained by the relentless heat, she'd hear the strains of Beethoven's piano concertas and, when she'd looked for her brother, she'd found him reclining on the porch with a glass of whiskey in his hand and his eyes closed. She knew how much he missed Da and she knew that his heart wasn't really in his vocation as a priest. In fact, she knew where his heart really was.

She glances at her reflection in the bedroom mirror. Her cheeks are flushed like Mammy's used to be when she'd been cooking and her hair is fluffy from the humidity. She looks at her watch. Just enough time to take a quick shower before they arrive.

The cuckoo clock chimes the hour as Mary and Damien step through the kitchen door. Da bought the clock for Mammy from *Martin Fennelly Antiques* when Damien was five and he used to oil it every two years until he died (which made it four times in all). He taught Damien how to oil and clean it, carefully and meticulously, which he did only twice before he left for university. He'd found the task therapeutic and distracting, never imagining that he would not be returning home after the last time he'd cleaned it, just before Mammy had written to say that Mary was going to marry Seamus.

He'd thought then that he would never recover from the hurt and debilitating depression which had followed and had tried to escape by drowning himself in his books and music and poetry. He'd read the words of Oriah Mountain Dreamer's *Night Tears 21* so many times that they were engraved in his brain: those '*small nocturnal creatures with sharp white teeth that silently gnaw at the edges of belly and heart*' and '*the wound that never heals*'. And, in the ensuing years in Africa, he would sometimes find himself wondering if he had 'ever touched the centre of his own sorrow and been opened by life's betrayals' 22, like Miss O'Leary had been or if, instead, he had become 'shrivelled and closed from fear of further pain'? Many years later he'd come across a new Mary Oliver poem.

> *That time*
> *I thought I could not*
> *go any closer to grief*
> *without dying*
> *I went closer,*
> *and I did not die.*
> *Surely God*
> *had his hand in this . . .* 23

He looks at Mary now, standing wide-eyed in front of the cuckoo clock, watching the little bird announce the hour and he feels a surge of tenderness towards her. He bends to kiss the nape of her neck. *I'm not shrivelled and closed,* he thinks, *I found the light within.* He puts his arms around her shoulders and pulls her up against his chest, burying his face in her hair. The little bird calls its final *coo-coo!* and retreats into its house.

Maeve appears at the bottom of the stairway.

'You used to oil that clock, Dami, when you were young. I remember you cleanin' it at the kitchen table . . . before you went to Trinners.'

'Aye, so I did,' says Damien, looking up at the clock, 'before I went to Trinners.'

Father Farwell

Father Farwell frowns as he scans the words in front of him. As if the church isn't dealing with enough problems, such as dwindling attendances, same-sex relationships, contraception, sexual abuse and a plethora of other scandals – now this shameful story about an Italian missionary priest in Africa, who chose the church over his son. He wipes his spectacles and reads on . . .

'I do really love you with all my heart and body', the priest wrote. 'You are the only one who is giving me, not only physical satisfaction, but a lot more. You are telling me and teaching me how beautiful it is to love and be together no matter the sacrifices we have to make for it'.

Soon after, Madeleine became pregnant.

'I accepted your decision regarding me, and yet I cannot accept your hiding behind the priesthood to refuse to help a child you helped bring into the world', she wrote. 'I do not know what you think he will think of you and of your priesthood and other priests when he grows up and learns how you treated him . . .'

Father Farwell wipes his spectacles again and leans back into his cracked leather chair, closing his eyes. 'Shameful!' he mutters, 'just utterly shameful and scandalous. May God have mercy on us all. The church must make atonement for its gross betrayal of trust.'

His discovery of Seamus Rafferty's dead body has left him feeling shattered and, he has to admit, rather ineffectual. Has he been deluded all these years, imagining that he is chosen to be God's conduit to man, Christ's representative on earth? Aren't all Christians supposed to be Christ's ambassadors, anyway? He opens his eyes and clasps his fingers over his soft spongy belly, pressing his thumbs together as he concentrates. His shirt buttons are straining and tufts of white hair are sprouting between the gaps. He's still haunted by the image of Seamus with his dead eyes fixed on the big gold crucifix at the altar. Did he find the peace that he was searching for in his last minutes, slumped over the altar rail? Could he not have helped the poor man out of the hell he was living in while he was still alive?

And what about poor Albert Donnelly? he thinks. *Right in front of my eyes and I didn't see it coming. I must make more effort to visit the estate, reach out to the poor lost souls; make sure Seamus' family receives assistance from Vincent de Paul. Ah, God have mercy on us all.*

He sighs as he wipes his spectacles again, holding them up to the light. He can hear footsteps on the wooden floor and turns, squinting, towards the door. He puts his spectacles on and peers at the large figure silhouetted in the door frame.

'Well, I'll be damned! Young Damien Donnelly. Welcome home, son.'

Damien

Father Farwell fixes his gaze on Damien as he recounts the events leading to his decision to leave the priesthood. *He's a handsome man, to be sure*, he thinks, *always was a fine-looking lad. Same complexion as his oul fella.*

He shows no emotion as Damien describes the torment which almost led to him taking his own life like his father before him. *Poor Albert*, thinks Father Farwell, *a fine, honest man he was. God only knows why he took such a drastic step. If only I'd been looking, I might have noticed his distress.* He focuses on the earnest face in front of him and listens intently, wiping his spectacles every few minutes, until Damien concludes his testimony. He sighs deeply and leans back into his chair, clasping his hands together on his soft stomach, rubbing his thumbs back and forth. On the desk beside him is a silver tray with an antique silver teapot, a polished silver milk jug, a bowl of sugar cubes and a plate of ginger biscuits.

A black-and-white cat alights softly onto the desk and the old priest pours some milk into a saucer, stroking the cat's back vigorously as it laps. 'There you go, Thomas, old boy,' he murmurs, 'come for your breakfast, have you?' Thomas purrs gratefully.

Father Farwell looks thoughtful and rubs his chin. 'You did not betray your own soul, Damien, son, and for that you have my deepest admiration and respect. It was not an easy decision for you to make and, to be sure, there will be murmuring and gossipmongering in the village. But you are strong and must hold your head up high. You have the integrity of your father, God bless his soul. He'd have been proud of you, Damien . . . he'd have been so proud.' He removes his spectacles and wipes his glistening face with a tissue, then stretches out his puffy, liver-spotted hand and clasps Damien's hand firmly. 'I have your job application before me, son. I've met with the school governing body and we've reached consensus. We'd like to appoint you as head of English and also offer you the position of pastoral director. You are more than qualified for such a post and you'd be an asset to the school. You may not be a priest, but you're still one of us and there is much work to be done.' He frowns and puts on his spectacles. 'God knows, there is much work to be done.'

Damien shakes his head in amazement and squeezes Father Farwell's hand.

'Thank you, Father. Thank you.'

He sits in silence, trying to digest the implication of the words he's just heard, inhaling the comforting aroma of old leather, books and tobacco: the unforgetteable smell of Da. The velvet wine-coloured curtains are reflected in the silver teapot as Father Farwell pours himself another cup of tea and refills Thomas' saucer with milk.

'Can I offer you another cup?' he asks Damien, 'or perhaps a ginger nut?'

Damien shakes his head as the priest dunks a biscuit into his teacup. 'My favourites,' he says, winking, 'my dear departed mater, God bless her soul, used to bake ginger biscuits. She used molasses – very healthy, full of iron . . .'

Damien smiles and gets to his feet, reaching out his hand. Thomas stops lapping and looks up at him quizzically. He shakes Father Farwell's hand once more and strides out of the peaceful, book-lined study, pausing at the door to look up at the ornately-framed painting on the wall directly in front of him.

'*Sacred Heart of Jesus*,' says Father Farwell, helping himself to another ginger nut, 'Pompeo Batoni, 1760.'

Miss O'Leary

The weather is still fine and warm when Damien steps out of the rectory. Father Farwell watches him cross the little garden and open the big heavy oak door into the church vestibule. *What a loss to the priesthood*, he thinks, sadly, stroking Thomas absent-mindedly, *but he's not lost to the church.*

Damien pauses before entering the nave with its marble black-and-white diamond-patterned floor, the rows of pews with embroidered kneelers, the magnificent stained glass windows and the small organ at the side. He lowers himself silently onto a wooden bench and looks around the church, breathing the unmistakeable smell of incense, flowers, prayer books and candles. Memories resurface of Da and Mammy in her peach-coloured hat in the front pew and Maeve and Mary in their white frocks and lace veils, kneeling for their first Communion with their tongues sticking out, while bony Mr Doyle played the organ softly in the background. He was no match for Dorothy. He surveys the altar and the imposing oak celebrant's chair – the seat of wisdom with its carved grapes and leaves and red velvet cushion where Father Farwell presided over Mass, and sometimes delivered the homily on the days when he was feeling peaky (which had become more frequent in latter years).

He turns towards the confessional where he'd made his first confession as a young lad. 'Bless me Father, for I have sinned . . . ' He'd been terrified then, never imagining that one day it would be him sitting in a confessional booth, imparting absolution to other terrified children. But Father Damien won't be administering the Sacrament of Penitence and Reconciliation ever again. He looks up at the marble statues, the beautiful stained glass windows and the weathered oak beams, then bows his head in prayer.

After several minutes he slips out of the cool, silent church into the bright sunny garden. He looks at his watch – Da's old watch which he'd never been able to wear until recently. What better time than now to take a walk to Miss O'Leary's cottage if, indeed, she still lives there? He'd once helped her carry some books home when he was sixteen. He furrows his brow in concentration. She must surely be nearly eighty by now?

He crosses over the little bridge and heads towards the old town centre, away from the busy shops and crowded sidewalks and turns into a narrow cobbled street, lined with uneven crooked walls and rickety staircases leading to tiny ancient dwellings. He stops and looks up at what he thinks is Miss O'Leary's house before climbing the stairs and pausing at the peeling blue door. He knocks loudly. The yellowing lace curtain ruffles before he hears slow, measured steps coming towards the door. It opens slowly and there, standing before him, is the now frail and bent, but unmistakeable form, of Miss O'Leary. She blinks as she looks up into Damien's face and for a moment she stares blankly at him, before a joyful smile of recognition starts to spread across her powdery, wrinkled face.

'Damien Donnelly!' she cries, 'is it yerself, son? You've come home!'

'Aye, I've come home, Miss O'Leary. I've come home.'

She spreads her arms out wide and Damien hesitates before embracing her frail little body, fearful of crushing her. She still smells of lavender and talcum powder and he can feel her bony shoulder blades poking through her grey hand-knitted cardigan. She ushers him in, pushing the door closed with her walking stick and indicates an old faded armchair, covered in white cat hair. She lowers herself gently onto a worn window seat and pushes aside an open newspaper which flutters to the floor.

Damien looks around the tiny cluttered room. There are some amateurish watercolours of Irish landscapes hanging crookedly on the uneven white-washed walls, a few carefully-embroidered cushion covers, mismatched pieces of furniture, faded rugs on the wooden floor and a blue and white china jug full of purple irises on the window sill. Above the stone fireplace is a rough-hewn timber mantel displaying faded black and white photographs, some framed and some tucked in behind others, alongside various china plates and saucers. In front of the fireplace is an old rocking chair with a tartan rug draped over it and a petit-point footstool. Against one wall there's a sagging bookcase and on every available surface there are books in ramshackle order. Damien cannot restrain himself and leaps up to examine them. There are tatty paperbacks with curled-up corners, travel books, biographies and heavy old encyclopedias amongst cracked and dry leather-bound classics which smell warm and dusty. He fingers the soft, delicate leather and the faded red binding of *The Collected Poems of Louis Macneice* and his eyes fall upon *New and Selected Poems of Mary Oliver*. He gently turns the worn pages as Miss O'Leary's frail, lilting voice recites behind him: '*Tell me, what is it you plan to do with your one wild and precious life?*' 16

He turns and smiles. Her pale milky eyes are shining, as she brushes away a lock of white hair which has come loose from its tortoiseshell comb. He looks down at the open book and reads aloud. '*I don't want to end up simply havin' visited this world 24 . . .*' He stops and looks up at her. 'It was you who taught me to love poetry, to love words, Miss O'Leary, and to be able to face death and betrayal and abandonment and find the light within.'

'Grace,' she says, softly, 'please call me Grace. You were always a special lad, Damien. You saw what other lads could not see, you had a wisdom beyond yer years. It brought great joy to me heart to share me passion wit you.' She peers at him through her spectacles. 'The church has gained another saint in you, so it has.'

Damien shakes his head and returns to his chair. Haltingly, he shares the events which had led to him leaving the priesthood. She listens intently, gazing at his honest open face, his brow furrowing with concentration, the way it used to do during her literature classes. Finally, he tells her about Mary and his desire to spend the rest of his life with her. As he concludes, Grace O'Leary wipes her eyes with her delicate lace handkerchief and stares past him, through the open window and into the distance, far beyond the houses and chimneys and trees. Damien is reminded of the words of Lord Byron: *He heard it, but he heeded not. His eyes were with his heart and that was far away.* [25]

She turns back to Damien and starts reciting in her familiar measured tones:

> *To live in this world*
> *you must be able*
> *to do three things:*
> *to love what is mortal;*
> *to hold it*
> *against your bones knowing*
> *your own life depends on it;*
> *and, when the time comes to let it go,*
> *to let it go.* [26]

She pauses, savouring the words, before she looks at Damien through her sad milky eyes. 'Marry her, Damien, son,' she says, softly, 'don't lose what you've found. Cherish every moment you have left together, for true love comes to so few of us.' She leans heavily on her cane and heaves herself up. 'And now, I'll be wettin' the tea.'

As he makes his way back to Maeve's house, Damien ponders over the life of Grace O'Leary. How different might it have been if Hugo Fothergill had been able to see beyond the physical and recognise the possibilities of a future with such a kind, empathic, sensitive soul? If she had been able to travel and visit the places that she could only see and dream about in her travel books, and experience other cultures?

Ah, well, her life may have been robbed of its potential, but it had been a life that had enriched his life and had left a lasting legacy. Wasn't that what Ralph Waldo Emmerson meant when he said: *To know even one life has breathed easier because you have lived. This is to have succeeded.* His thoughts turn to Mary, waiting eagerly for him to return, and to Maeve and Fearghus and the good news he has to share with them all. He quickens his pace as he hurries towards his new home.

From her front window, Grace O'Leary watches Damien make his way over the cobbled street with his hands in his pockets, deep in thought. She remembers, as though it were yesterday, his eager face in the classroom, soaking up every word she spoke and Miss Corbishley-Smythe, the librarian, telling her how young Damien Donnelly would spend hours in the library poring over reference books about poets and artists. She remembers, too, his angst-filled poems after the loss of his father and how she'd cried when she'd read them in the solitude of her bedroom. They'd reminded her of the awkward, shy, heart-filled poems she'd written to Hugo in the days when she'd believed that true love knew no obstacles or distance.

She wipes her eyes with her lace handkerchief and returns to her chair by the hearth.

Damien

He pulls back the curtain and sighs with relief. The sun is shining in shafts of brilliance, filtering between the rooftops and trees, over the hedgerows and the fields beyond.

He hums as he dresses, buttoning his best shirt – the blue and white checked one that Dorothy had given him last Christmas. From downstairs he can hear the muffled drone of the tumble drier and the clanging of pots and pans, followed by the spraying of water running into the cistern of the lavatory under the stairs. Maeve's voice carries up to the bedroom.

'I'll be headin' into town to do the messages now, Dami. It's a fine day out there today.'

He shouts his farewell to Maeve and grabs a banana on his way out of the kitchen door.

The rows of orange, yellow and pink houses along the street look newly washed after the rain and the village looks almost postcard-perfect. Even the cars outside each house are parked neatly in a row on the curb. Far ahead in the distance he can just make out the back view of his sister, with her thickening waist, bustling along, clutching her basket. How like Mammy she has become. He strides on towards town, crosses over the little bridge which straddles the gently flowing stream and pops into O'Malley's grocery store.

'Damien, lad! Is it yerself? Haven't seen ya in donkeys, man,' says Mr O'Malley, offering his hand. 'Good to see ya, son. You visiting yer sister?' He glances through the window. 'Tis a soft day today, tank God.' He's wearing a striped butcher's apron and his spectacles are resting on his forehead; a pencil is tucked behind his ear and tufts of grey hair are sprouting from his ears and nostrils. Behind him are shelves laden with tinned beans, jars of instant coffee and mayonnaise, jams and marmalades, boxes of Paracetemol and Benadryl and assorted bottles of wine.

'It is, to be sure,' says Damien, 'perfect day for a picnic.'

He loads his purchases into a big sturdy canvas bag, decorated with camels, which Maeve had bought on a trip to Dubai several years ago: a bottle of Prosecco, a loaf of crusty white bread, a slab of aged mature cheddar and two chocolate brownies. The door flies open and Gladys Foley lurches in, dragging a little shopping trolley behind her. Strands of grey hair are escaping from a scarf tied under her chin and beads of perspiration are running down her brow.

'Ah, tis cruel warm out dere,' she sighs, wiping her forehead, 'tea is da only ting for dis heat. Only last month it was so feckin' bitter out and sure, didn't ya know dat everyone was gettin' sick because of da feckin' wedder? Dat wind would go right troo ya for a short cut . . . '

Damien puts his head down and ducks out of her vision. 'Catch ya later!' he calls to Mr O'Malley, as the door bangs shut behind him.

He heads off towards Mary's cottage, slinging the bag as he walks. The sidewalk trembles slighty as the bus rumbles past, leaving the odorous smell of diesel in the air. He passes the hedgerows covered in lingering brownish blossoms and breathes the gentle fragrance of magnolia floating from the trellises of the houses along the narrow street. Finally, he arrives at Mary's cottage and approaches the front door. He pauses at the porch, reliving for a moment that glorious, unforgettable night when he had first kissed her. He looks up at the worn old lamp that had illuminated her beautiful face and smiles as he knocks on the door.

It opens immediately. Mary is standing in the hallway, dressed in white shorts and a blue floral blouse. Her hair is tied up with a matching blue ribbon and on her feet are a pair of espadrilles. Damien catches his breath at the sight of her, puts the canvas bag on the floor and embraces her in a hug. She smells of fresh-cut flowers, of roses and lilies, and he inhales the familiar sweet scent of her. Rufus jumps lightly from the sofa and rubs himself against their legs, purring contentedly.

'We haven't forgotten you, Rufie,' says Mary, bending to stroke him. Her thighs are firm and smooth and golden and Damien looks admiringly at her shapely legs.

'Shall we be off then, Mary Rose? It's a perfect day for a picnic.'

She smiles up at him and touches his face. 'Oh, Dami, I'm so happy. I don't think I could ever be happier.'

Damien and Mary

Mary is feeling a little apprehensive about the prospect of returning to the oak tree where she had once witnessed her husband and Rosheen Murphy in *flagrante delicto*. Not that she'd been surprised or shocked and it had given her the evidence she'd needed to divorce Seamus, but it had sullied her memories of the happy summers she and Maeve and Damien used to spend there.

She doesn't mention it to Damien though, and they set off down the road, hand in hand, the canvas bag swaying back and forth in unison with their steps. They pass the pubs, boutique shops and galleries on the busy, narrow, winding street and turn down the quiet country lane where the landscape suddenly changes. Stunning pink wildflowers and bright yellow lichen adorn the lush green fields stretching for miles in the distance and sheep are grazing contentedly in the meadows. They cross over a low stone wall and Damien helps Mary negotiate the old rusted fence, avoiding the nettles the way he used to do when they were young. And suddenly, there before them, shimmering in the sun, is the crystal blue water of the stream and the huge gnarled roots of the old oak tree.

'The Magic Faraway Tree,' sighs Mary, gazing up into its wide spreading branches.

They settle down on a smooth patch of ground and lean back against the trunk. Pale rays of sunlight are filtering through the branches. She sighs contentedly and turns to Damien.

'Dami, do you remember when we used to eat blackers and our lips and tongues would turn purple?'

He smiles. 'Sure I do. And remember when you dared us to jump into the stream?' He looks into her shining blue eyes and runs his finger over her dimples. 'The sight of you in your underwear, your white panties with daisies embroidered on them . . . I'd never seen such a vision of beauty before. That was when I knew that I loved you, Mary Rose. You stole my heart away complete.'

She blushes and presses his hand against her cheek. 'I felt the same. I thought you were the most beautiful sight I had ever seen.' She looks into his eyes. 'I still do.'

He kisses her tenderly before slowly emptying the bag of its contents. Then he reaches into his pocket and gets down on one knee. 'Mary Rose O'Mara,' he says, his voice breaking, 'I love you with all my heart. Will you marry me?' He holds up an antique gold ring with a cabochon opal at the centre, surrounded by seven pearls. 'This was Mammy's ring. Da gave it to her for their seventh anniversary. He saved for it for years.'

Mary gives a little shriek. 'Oh, Dami! Oh, yes, yes, yes!' She flings her arms around his neck and kisses him on his forehead, on his eyes, on his cheeks and finally on his mouth. He takes her left hand and gently slides the ring onto her finger. Sunlight flashes onto the stones, diffracting them into a million colours and Mary stares at the ring in amazement. 'It's beautiful, Dami. I love it. You've just made me the happiest lass in the world.'

He pours the champagne into two plastic goblets and they drink to their future, to the years they will spend together, to the dreams they thought they had lost. They share the bread and cheese and the brownies and lie back against the tree trunk, patting their extended bellies, like they usd to do when they were lying in front of the fire after Christmas dinner. Slowly, a smile starts to spread across Mary's face and she leaps up and starts pulling her top over her head, shouting, 'Dare you!' as she runs towards the stream. Damien follows her, throwing off his shirt and jeans and they plunge together into the freezing water.

As they dry off in the sun Mary lies still on her stomach, watching the colours changing on her opal ring. Seven pearls for seven years. Damien studies her intently. Her wet hair is cascading down her shoulders and when the sun's rays dance across it, it looks midnight blue, just like it did when she was a little girl. Her skin feels as soft as velvet as he runs his fingers down the nape of her neck and into the little hollow at its base. The long line of her neck flows smoothly into her silky shoulders where drops of water glisten and roll like little sparkling glass beads. The line continues down her spine, into the curve of her narrow waist and flows out again over her hips and rounded buttocks. Damien is reminded of a painting called *Rokeby Venus* by the Spanish artist, Velazquez, which he'd seen in a library book when he was a teenager: Venus, the goddess of love, reclining languidly on her bed, as she gazes into a mirror, held by her son, Cupid. The sweeping curves of her body had enraptured the sixteen-year-old Damien. He'd guiltily put the book back on the shelf, blushing furiously, when he'd noticed Miss Corbishley-Smythe watching him over her spectacles.

'Mary,' he says, his voice husky with emotion, 'let's not wait any longer to get married. Let's do it tomorrow.'

'Tomorrow?' cries Mary, her eyes wide with surprise. 'Are you serious, Dami? A wedding tomorrow? You're crazy! We just got engaged!'

'Next Saturday, then?'

She stares at him in disbelief, shaking her head.

'I don't want to wait for the rest of our lives to begin. We've waited long enough, Mary. All the years we've been apart, the longing . . . I just want to be with you now. For you to be my wife.'

'Ah, Dami, I do so love you and my greatest joy is to be your wife.' She flings her arms in the air. 'Oh, what the heck! If we can plan a wedding by next Saturday, lets do it.'

He sweeps her wet hair into a ponytail and kisses her on the nose. 'You're a fine wee thing, Mary Rose O'Mara. I can't wait.'

They gather their belongings together and start to make their way home. Suddenly Mary stops and runs back to the spot where they had been lying. She bends and retrieves a reddening oak leaf which she tucks into the band of her shorts. She looks up, and in the distance, caught on the barbed wire fence, is a piece of torn black lace, fluttering gently in the breeze.

Maeve

Maeve is sitting at her desk, enjoying the fresh breeze blowing lightly through the open window. The sun is still warm in the soft evening light and the smell of honeysuckle lingers in the air. The last of the late afternoon traffic has finally subsided and childrens' voices float up from the street below. The bookcase trembles as a heavy lorry rumbles past and the smell of honeysuckle is briefly erased by the smell of burning oil.

At the end of the road she can see two figures walking hand in hand. As they get closer she recognises Damien and Mary, deep in conversation. She smiles as she watches them turn to one another, grinning and laughing, their faces glowing and golden from the sun. Mary's hair looks wet and tangled. *They must've been swimmin' in the stream,* thinks Maeve, *Lord knows, it's been fierce warm enough today.* She feels a sudden pang of jealousy as she watches them together, so absorbed in one another, oblivious to their surroundings.

When she was a teenager, Maeve used to dream of meeting a noble, rakish, handsome young man, like the heroes in the love-laced Barbara Cartland novels she used to hide from Damien. She would imagine herself in a passionate embrace with an open-shirted, muscled lothario or wrapped in the arms of a swarthy Spanish lover like the one on the cover of *Love is Triumphant.* Oh, she does love

Fearghus but she was never 'in love' with him in the way she thought all brides were supposed to be. She'd never felt weak at the knees, full of throbbing passion and desire, or yearned for Fearghus when he wasn't with her, but she'd always known that he would be in her corner and would treat her with kindness and respect. She does understand that he finds it difficult to express his emotions and is undemonstrative (except when he's had a few pints of Guiness) and, after all, isn't 'loving' more permanent than being 'in love'?

The front door opens and Damien calls from the bottom of the staircase.

'Anybody home?'

'Aye,' Maeve responds, 'it's meself. I'll be down now, so I will. Let's be wettin' the tea then, shall we?'

'Not tea, Maeve. Champagne.'

Maeve comes flying down the stairs and Mary holds out her hand, flashing the opal ring.

Maeve shrieks. 'Engaged? G'way outta that! Oh, glory be!' She throws her arms around Mary and then Damien. 'Fearghus!' she shouts, 'C'mere from outside. Dami and Mary have some news for you!'

Fearghus appears at the kitchen door in his flat cap and wellies with a pitchfork in his hand. 'What's the craic?'

'Look!' shrieks Maeve, holding up Mary's hand.

'Yer feckin' coddin' me!' says Fearghus, a broad smile settling across his face. He removes his cap and wipes his grubby hands on his overall before he embraces the couple in a hug.

'Fetch the champers, Fearghus, love,' says Maeve, beaming, 'that bottle we've been savin' since New Year. Remember we said there'll be somethin' to celebrate this year?'

They gather in the front room while Fearghus pops the champagne. He lifts his glass in a toast to the happy couple. 'Fair play, mate!' he says, turning to Damien, 'fair play.'

Damien takes a deep sip before clearing his throat. 'Now, I know this'll come as a shock to you both, but we want to get married next Saturday,' he says, glancing at Mary.

'Saturday?' says Maeve, startled, 'did you say Saturday, Dami? Ah, sure, we can't plan a weddin' by Saturday!'

'Just a civil union at the registry office, followed by a service of blessin' by Father Farwell . . . if he's willing,' says Damien, smiling at Mary. He takes her hand. 'Bound together by God till we die.'

'Oh, it's all so sudden!' cries Maeve, shaking her head and flinging her arms in the air. 'You're an awful snake, Dami, not tellin' me. But, hey, there's no time to waste now. We can have the blessin' here at the house . . . how are we goin' to notify everyone? If you want guests, that is?' She thumps herself on the head. 'Ah, Maeve McCarthy, yer gettin' ahead o' yerself again.'

'Just tell Fatima Patel and Ma Dooley,' says Fearghus, 'and the whole effin' village will be here.'

Maeve laughs and turns to her husband. 'Fearghus, love, you and the boys will have to take Dami to Patrick Street tomorrow, buy him some new clothes.' She takes a sip of champagne and smothers a burp. 'Take him to Paddy O'Sullivan for a good haircut; and buy him some new specs while you're about it.' She turns back to Damien. 'You can't be seen wearin' those old banjaxed tortoiseshell relics, Dami!' She takes another sip and turns to Mary. 'Ah, I'm rarin' to go now, Mary! You and me will head off to town tomorrow, find a nice frock for you.' Her face is glowing and her cheeks are flushed. She raises her glass again.

'I'm delira and excira now! Just wait til the lads get home! They'll be gobsmacked to be sure!'

Mary

She drifts slowly out of a deep sleep, stretching her arms and rubbing her eyes as she looks around her. She's back in her bedroom. There's the tallboy in front of her, the bookcase overflowing with books and the framed photographs of Daddy and a much younger Ma and the girls and Damien smiling happily into the camera lense. It had all been a dream . . .

She and Damien had been running barefoot over a bridge which straddled a still, mirror-like pool with water lilies floating on the surface. They'd run towards a gate which had swung open and, on either side of them were green fields and a graveyard. Row upon row of smooth, white, polished marble tombstones rose from the grass like sentinels keeping vigil, guarding the dead to ensure that they forever rest in peace. As they ran, Mary could see the names engraved on some of the tombstones: Frank O'Mara, Marion O'Mara, Albert Donnelly, Agnes Donnelly and the last, freshly-dug grave of Seamus Rafferty, piled high with rich red soil. They had run towards a huge oak tree with broad, sturdy branches spreading across the sky and a ladder leading up into its boughs. They'd climbed it, eating blackberries, and, sitting on the outspread branches, clapping in unison, were the familiar figures of Sister Evangelina with her Scotty dog, Angus, Miss O'Leary, waving her lace handkerchief, Father Farwell and the Patels.

Finally, right at the top, were Fearghus, Maeve, young Damien and Brendan, all smiling with black lips. Damien and Mary had stood hand-in-hand on the top rung of the ladder and looked out at the landscape stretching for miles in the distance. Damien had turned to Mary and pointed. 'This is eternity, Mary Rose.'

In the moment between sleep and consciousness, she had been aware of a feeling of anticipated excitement, the way she used to feel when she woke on Christmas Day and knew that something wonderful was about to unfold. Now she's wide awake and is gradually realising that today is going to be the happiest day of her life.

She leaps out of bed and runs to the window, pulling back the curtain. She frowns. The dark sky is awash with various shades of grey, with wispy white clouds of candy floss dashed across it like the strokes of a paint brush. 'Ah, well, it's only spittin',' she mutters. 'It's goin' to be a perfect day, I just know it is.'

The village is still asleep. Office workers are having a lie-in, there are no lights glowing in front rooms and no traffic on the roads. Even Rufus stays curled up next to Mary's crumpled pillow, his green eyes watching her intently. She pulls on her bathrobe and creeps downstairs to make a cup of coffee, then returns to her warm bed and props herself up against the pillows. Is Damien still asleep, or has he too woken early to marvel at the destination they have finally reached and to contemplate the unfolding joy that surely lies before them?

She leans back and closes her eyes, remembering those happy years when Daddy and Maeve's mammy were still alive; when life had a predictable, reassuring rhythm and home had meant Damien and Maeve and the smell of warm bread and lamb stew, of cinnamon and toasted marshmallows and a crackling fire in winter. She'd had such innocent dreams of love then, of living happily ever after, especially after Damien had kissed her under the porch light. And then, unbidden and unexpected, like a thief in the night, had come the dreadful incident that had catapulted them into years of grief and heartache and mourning for what might have been. But now their painful journey has reached a happy destination.

She whispers a prayer of thanks to the one who saved her and restored what she thought had been lost to her forever, then takes a sip of coffee and reaches for the book on her bedside table. *The Selected Poems of W B Yeats.* An old, paper-thin, brown oak leaf wafts onto her chest and crumples into tiny transparent flecks. Still wedged between the pages, is the new coppery-red leaf that she retrieved the previous weekend. She smiles. Strength, endurance, faith and eternity, that's what Sister Evangelina said. She re-reads the inscription on the fly leaf, written in Damien's neat cursive handwriting.

I have spread my dreams under your feet;
*Tread softly because you tread on my dreams.*6

Through the open curtains the grey sky is starting to dissolve and patches of blue are emerging in its place, as the sun starts pushing through the clouds. A chorus of birdsong breaks the dawn and the smell of coffee and bacon floats across the street. A dog barks and Rufus looks up anxiously. 'Time to get ready now, Rufie,' says Mary, stroking his back, 'it's gonna to be a fine day after all. Maeve will be comin' to dress me soon.'

Rufus rolls over onto his back, exposing his white belly, with his legs straight up in the air. His magical green eyes are sparkling like emeralds, as he stares intently at Mary and purrs softly.

Damien

He wakes to a cacophony of household sounds: the metallic clattering of pots and pans, the spluttering of water from the bathroom faucet and the hum of the washing machine. In the distance he can hear the drone of traffic from the motorway. The smell of freshly-ground coffee wafts up the stairs. He looks at his bedside clock – six thirty. Maeve is awake early today, bustling about like Mammy, preparing the wedding feast.

He'd been deeply touched to see the pure joy in his sister's face when he and Mary had shared their news and her genuine delight that Mammy's opal ring was now on Mary's finger. And even reticent Fearghus had failed to conceal his pleasure. He and the boys had taken Damien to Patrick Street and bought him a tailored grey suit and a crisp white shirt, a pair of black leather loafers, two sweaters and a pair of Levis. Next, they'd visited the barber shop and Paddy O'Sullivan had trimmed his hair. 'Sure, yer in need of a bazzer!' Paddy had exclaimed, 'ya look like a feckin' bogger, Damien! Where ya been, lad? Out in Africa?' They'd celebrated at O'Connor's with Guiness and braised rabbit pie, while a fiddler played *Danny Boy* and *Molly Malone*.

He lies back in bed for a few moments of reflection. He could never, in a million years, have imagined that he, Damien Donnelly, former priest, would be back in Ireland with his beloved sister, about to marry the love of his life. He pictures her sweet face, her big china-blue eyes, her full red lips, her black tousled hair and her clear, smooth, creamy skin. *Today, Mary Rose, you will be mine.*

All the years of sadness and despair, when he'd thought to end his life like Da have now been drowned in a sea of such happiness and contentment, he can hardly find the words to describe how he feels this morning. He takes out his new spectacles and opens his book of poetry at the page he had marked with the old photograph of him and the girls brandishing their tennis racquets triumphantly: the photograph Seamus took.

> *Have you ever felt for anything*
> *such wild love*
> *do you think there is anywhere, in any language,*
> *a word billowing enough*
> *for the pleasure*
> *that fills you?* 27

'No word,' he says softly, 'no word in any language.'

He closes the book, reaches for the pad and pen on the bedside table and begins to write.

My dear Cynthia . . . he pauses, frowning as he tries to put into words what he needs to say. . . *By now you will have been told that I have left the priesthood (God knows I wanted to tell you myself). But there is something else I need to tell*

you. You were right when you said I was hiding a
deep sadness – you always were so perceptive . .
.

He finishes the letter and pictures her opening it. How will she react to his news? With sadness, no doubt, but also with happiness for him because he has found love and Cynthia knows what it means to love. He tucks the letter into an envelope, slips out of bed and kneels at the beside, bowing his head in prayer. In the distance a rooster is crowing and downstairs the cuckoo clock is chiming the hour.

The Wedding

Maeve adds the finishing touches to Mary's outfit and places a garland of white flowers and ivy onto her head like a crown; her hair is loose and tumbles down her shoulders in shiny ringlets. 'Ah, Mary,' she sighs, 'you look like a goddess.' She hugs her friend and brushes away the tears that have been forming so easily the past week.

They'd had such fun searching for the perfect dress for Mary: something simple and whimsical, lacy and flowing, and had finally found it at *Needle and Thread* in the lane behind Patrick Street. They'd whooped with joy when Mary had tried it on and had celebrated over coffee and cream scones at The Blackberry Tearoom. They'd talked with wonderment about the events that had lead to this moment, about their joy at being reunited with Damien and their dreams for the future; they'd laughed at the memories of their antics as school girls and they'd cried because Mammy and Frank were not there to witness the union.

'Ah, but Mammy would have been so sad and disappointed about Dami leavin' the priesthood,' Maeve had said, licking cream off her lips. 'She'd already borne the whisperin' about Da, so perhaps it's better she's not here. But Mary, my love, how brave can a man be to be true to himself? Our Dami always had integrity and unwaverin' principles, just like Da. He's an honourable man, so he is.'

'How did Shakespeare put it?' Mary said, closing her eyes as she tried to remember the words Sister Evangelina had drummed into them.

This above all: to thine own self be true,
And it must follow, as the night the day,
Thou canst not then be false to any man. 28

'Away wi' you and your *poo-etry,* Mary!' Maeve had said, shaking her head, 'how do you even remember those verses? You and Dami – two peas in a pod!' She'd paused, gazing out of the window. 'Ah, well, they'll forgive and forget soon enough – there's always a new story. I can just see Ma Dooley whisperin' outside Patel's with her hand over her mouth: *C'mere till I tell ye* . . . God knows, I've been on the receivin' end myself.'

Now Mary is standing in front of the mirror, looking like a Grecian princess. The lace skirt of her simple white gown flows softly from an empire waistband of tiny pearl-centred flowers and her smooth shoulders and arms are enhanced by the sleevelees V-necked dress. Maeve places a little bunch of white garden roses and seeded eucalyptus in her hand. The tallboy trembles as the number 10 bus rumbles past and Fearghus pulls up and starts hooting.

The pale blue Toyota Corolla has two white ribbons attached rather clumsily to the bonnet and they're already starting to sag. Fearghus is seated proudly behind the wheel in his only suit, his ginger beard washed and trimmed and his hair slicked back with hair cream so that it looks almost crimson. Damien alights from the passenger door in his new grey suit and white shirt with a red rose in his lapel. His eyes are shining and his face is glowing as he steps into Mary's front door.

Maeve is standing proudly at the bottom of the staircase dressed in an apricot silk suit, with a feathery fascinator perched in her hair. 'Ah, Dami, you look so handsome!' she exclaims, hugging her brother, 'just like a prince.'

He looks up to see his bride descending the staircase, just as he had done twenty years ago when Mary had appeared in her red dress. He had been mesmerised then and is spellbound now, frozen to the spot. His eyes meet hers as she steps slowly down towards him and it feels again as though everything is moving in slow motion. He wants to freeze this moment for ever but he puts out his hand and she takes it in hers and they kiss. 'You are the most beautiful sight I have ever seen, Mary Rose,' he says, 'and I will love you all my life.'

Maeve hastily captures the moment with her cellphone: the bride and groom with their fingers entwined and their eyes locked in an intimate embrace. She wipes away the tears that are coursing down her cheeks and smudging her mascara, leaving black streaks which are melding into her rouge, making her look like a *Pierrot* doll.

Fearghus bows as he opens the back door for Mary while Damien helps Maeve into the front seat. The Corolla turns into the street and they purr through the village, waving like royalty to the old men tipping their caps and the women outside their front doors, fluttering their handkerchiefs. Maeve dabs at the tears that are welling up again and places her hand on Fearghus' knee. He turns to her and smiles lovingly, placing his pale freckled hand on hers.

The Reception

The wedding guests are gathered in the front room, eagerly awaiting the arrival of the bride and groom. Father Farwell has graciously agreed to officiate at the blessing ceremony, although he would have preferred it to be in the church. For a brief moment he wonders how it must feel to be betrothed to a woman and not to the church. *Ah, well, to be sure, the Lord has called us all to different roles. There are few who can subjugate the flesh like me and God knows, even fewer entering the holy priesthood nowadays,* he thinks, sadly, wiping his spectacles with a paper napkin and looking around the room. *There's Donal Dooley with his ma. She'll be spreading the news around the village before the cock crows. And the Patels (pity they are Hindus, but there we are); and poor little Miss O'Leary with her lace handkerchief; a lame fella I don't recognise and the two McCarthy lads, getting so big . . . haven't seen them at the Mass lately.*

They look away anxiously as Father Farwell bears down on them.

Fatima Patel is wearing a shiny gold silk sari wrapped around her waist and over her shoulder. A roll of brown flesh is exposed around her middle and her greying black hair is scraped into a bun with some loose oily strands hanging limply on her face. She and Ma Dooley are engaged in conversation and Fatima's shrill voice carries across the room.

'He was always a good boy, Damien. Respectful, very honest. And Mary, a sweet girl. Wasted on that gobshite, Seamus . . . '

Ma Dooley is wondering if it's true that Fatima uses mayonnaise to condition her hair. She purses her lips and leans towards her. 'Divorced,' she whispers, pursing her lips.

'No, not divorced, Mrs Dooley. She's a widow now,' replies Fatima, smiling.

Miss O'Leary wipes her brow with her handkerchief and pulls her bony little shoulders back as she makes her way unsteadily across the room to the two women. 'Heaven is surely smilin' today,' she says, 'God knows, they both deserve happiness.'

Ma Dooley shakes her head. 'Don't know what this world is comin' to. A fallen priest marryin' a divorcee. God have mercy on us all.' Her hand flies to her forehead and she makes the sign of the cross. Father Farwell is talking to Maeve's two bored-looking sons and she heads towards them. *I'm surprised he's even here*, she thinks, shaking her head, *must be gettin' soft in his old age.*

Mr Patel turns to Miss O'Leary. Is that lavender he's smelling? 'Fatima and I, we are honoured to be here on such a *suspicious* day. Damien is a good man, always was kind and respectful as a lad. Helped me in the shop. Honest and trustworthy. Looked after his ma and sister after his oul fella passed. That was very sad. Very sad.' He frowns and shakes his head.

'But he was strong too, protected the weak. I well remember the day he smashed Seamus Rafferty into my vegetable display for teasing little Ronnie Watson.' He chuckles. His eyes crinkle at the corners and the wrinkles in his forehead fold into furrows. 'Fatima, she was so angry, but not with Damien. She always loved that boy.'

Miss O'Leary smiles. 'Aye, to be sure, I always knew he was destined for great things.'

The sound of hooting alerts the guests and they make their way to the front porch. The Corolla pulls up at the kerb, the ribbons now dangling limply from the bonnet. Fearghus and Maeve alight and open the back doors and Damien and Mary emerge, looking radiant.

Maeve sighs. *Just like Prince Charming and Cinderella alightin' from the pumpkin coach . . .* She starts singing, softly, 'no matter how your heart is grievin', if you keep on believin', the dream that you wish can come true.'29 She watches Mary and Damien make their entrance to the claps and cheers of the assembled guests. *Real love stories should always have a good old happy endin'*, she thinks, smiling with satisfaction.

Father Farwell clears his throat. 'Time for congratulations after the blessing, folks,' he says, 'would you take your seats, please, so that we can commence.'

Damien and Mary stand, hand in hand, in front of Father Farwell as he leads them in a short service of dedication. He concludes with the Song of Solomon, reciting in his rich, deep voice. *'Many waters cannot quench love, neither can floods drown it. If a man offered for love all the wealth of his house, it would be utterly scorned. I am my beloved's and my beloved is mine. 30* I now declare you husband and wife before God.'

Damien cups Mary's face in his hands and kisses her tenderly while Maeve sobs more tears of joy. Miss O'Leary wipes her eyes with her lace handkerchief, Ma Dooley sniffs and rummages in her white plastic handbag for a tissue and Fatima lets out a whoop of joy. Mr Patel turns to her and puts his finger to his lips. 'Be hush, now, Fatima. Be hush.'

Feargus and the boys start popping champagne corks, while Maeve hurries to remove the nets covering the assortment of sandwiches, meat balls, devilled eggs and Fatima's homemade samoosas. In the centre of the table is a large vanilla sponge cake with a little plastic bride and groom perched on the top.

They drink a toast to the newly-weds and laughter and music erupt from the house, spilling out into the street. Miss O'Leary hugs Mary and then Damien and looks up into his beaming face, her eyes sparkling behind her spectacles. 'You'll be comin' to see me again now, won't you, son? Bring yer lovely wife. Sure, the college is blessed to have a new English teacher the likes o' yerself.' She hands him a gift, wrapped in tissue paper with a card tucked inside it.

Damien opens it carefully and turns, smiling, to Mary. *'Rules for the Dance.* Mary Oliver. Well, I learned from the best, Miss . . . Grace,' he says, 'Grace. Your legacy will live on.'

A lame, sandy-haired, freckle-faced man limps up to Damien and extends his hand. Damien looks deep into his eyes, searching for a flicker of recognition. 'It's Ronnie,' says the lame man, 'Ronnie Watson.'

'G'wan!' says Damien, embracing him in a hug, 'wee Ronnie Watson? Sure, you've grown to be a fine young man. Look at the height o'you! Ah, it's grand to see you again.'

Brendan and young Damien produce a CD of Irish reels and jigs and the party starts to liven up. Mr Patel is dancing with Ma Dooley. Her large bosom is heaving and her fascinator is protruding like antler horns. Mary is dancing with young Damien, her skirt swirling to the music and her hair flowing around her glowing face. Miss O'Leary is dancing with her favourite pupil (heel toe, heel toe), her thin little arm entwined with Damien's, and Father Farwell is dancing with Fatima Patel. Her sari is swaying and shimmering as the roll of flesh around her middle jiggles and Father Farwell, his cheeks flushed and rosy, wipes his spectacles and twirls Fatima around like a ballerina on a musical box.

Fearghus grabs his wife's hand. 'C'mere, Maeve. I have a surprise for you.'

She look startled, as he leads her up the staircase.

'Wait here and close yer eyes.'

He returns from the bedroom.

'Now, open them.'

He gently places a little bundle of white fluff into her hands. 'Meet Molly Malone,' he says, his eyes brimming with tears.

Molly gazes up at Maeve with her big, wet, droopy eyes and snuggles into her chest.

'Ah, Fearghus!' cries Maeve, gazing at the puppy adoringly, 'my heart is meltin'. She looks just like Dottie when she was a puppy.'

'Aye,' says Fearghus, blinking away his tears. 'Same family. Got her from O'Keeffe.' He looks embarrassed and his cheeks flush as he continues. 'You deserve a new dog, Maeve. You deserve a lotta things I can't give you. You've been the anchor in my life; in the boys' lives too.'

She reaches out one hand. 'C'mere to me, Fearghus, love,' she says, hugging him awkwardly to her bosom, smelling the Guiness on his breath. 'I couldn't have done it without you; you've always been my rock.' She kisses him softly on his cheek. 'Now, shall we introduce Molly Malone to the weddin' party?'

They make their way downstairs where the music is getting louder and faster. Molly Malone is passed from guest to guest, with much 'oohing' and 'aahing' until she is whisked away by young Damien. Brendan furtively slurps a few swigs of champagne and turns up the volume, shaking his head at the old codgers throwing shapes on the dance floor.

Midnight approaches and the cuckoo clock chimes the hour, as the party comes to an end. Mary retrieves her bouquet from the tumbler of water on the dresser and the guests assemble behind her. She tosses it over her shoulder and there's a gasp as it lands in Miss O'Leary's trembling little hands, spraying tiny drops of water into the air. She looks up in astonishment, her pale milky eyes shining behind her thick lenses. Father Farwell wipes his spectacles with his handkerchief and Maeve wipes away another tear with a paper napkin.

They gather at the front door to give Damien and Mary a rousing send-off, shouting *Slainte!* in unison. Fearghus ushers the newlyweds into the Corolla which is now festooned with tin cans clattering from the back bumper and balloons floating from the windows. The hooter sounds, *parp-parp!* and he punches the air, as the car disappears around the bend.

Father Farwell assists Mr Patel and Fatima into his old lime green Mazda and settles himself behind the wheel, adjusting his spectacles which are glinting under the light of the lamp post. He buckles his seat belt and the car jerks away into the darkness. Ronnie Watson links his arm with Miss O'Leary's and together they totter unsteadily towards the bus stop, leaning heavily on their canes, just as the last bus pulls up.

Ma Dooley watches them from the sidewalk and wipes her eyes. *Ah, well, life isn't always what it seems. Nobody's perfect. God knows, we all need love. And grace. We all need grace.*

Damien and Mary

As the Corolla turns into the lane Mary turns to Damien and sighs happily. 'Ah, it's been such a perfect, wondrous day, Dami.'

Damien smiles at his bride. 'A brilliant, fantastic day!'

'Aye,' says Fearghus, nodding his head, 'it has, to be sure. A splendid day. Haven't had such craic in donkeys.'

He observes the couple making their way to the front door of Mary's cottage and watches Damien take Mary's hand under the porch light, blinking back the tears that have suddenly appeared out of nowhere. Perhaps Maeve is right: she's always believed in fairytales and happy endings. He smiles as he revs the car's engine and makes his way home to his sweet, practical, dependable wife, resolving to be more affectionate in the future.

Damien pauses under the porch light, picturing again the vision of seventeen-year-old Mary in her red dress, smelling of fresh flowers and apples, remembering the feel of her soft skin under his fingers. He takes her into his arms and kisses her passionately, just as he had done all those years ago when he had known that he would love her for the rest of his life. He gazes with wonderment into her face and their eyes lock before he pushes the door open and carries her over the threshold. As he lowers her gently to the floor his eyes fall on the photograph on the dresser in front of him, the picture that Seamus had taken more than twenty years ago of Mary, Maeve and Damien triumphantly brandishing their tennis racquets. Rufus appears silently at their feet and starts rubbing himself against their ankles, in and out, in and out, like a figure of eight. Eternity.

'We found our way back, Mary Rose,' says Damien softly, 'true love stories never have endings.'

Cynthia

Far away, in a Chinese built mission hospital in Africa, a rooster crows and a red-faced baby boy utters a piercing, shrill cry as Dr Ncube delivers him into the world. Cynthia clutches her daughter's hand as tears of joy pour down her face. 'Welcome to the family, little Michael,' she whispers, 'your grandpa would have been so proud.'

Five minutes later, Cynthia Grace utters her first cry and is placed gently into the arms of her exhausted but elated mother beside her twin brother.

Sunlight is streaming into the ward when Cynthia leaves her sleeping daughter and her twin babies and steps into the cold dark corridor with the shiny, enamel-painted walls – bottle-green under the dado rail and cream above. Past the nurses' stations, through the swing doors with the frosted glass panels and down the ox-blood red staircase. The same route she'd taken when she'd left Michael unconscious in his hospital bed, attached to tubes and machines, his life ebbing away, while his precious little Emma slept peacefully in her Cinderella coach bed, oblivious to the fact that she would never see her father again. But now his seed will live on in his grandchildren and in the souls he left behind.

She emerges from the hospital entrance into the carpark with its gravelly, uneven surface and acacia trees with white-painted trunks that look like short white skirts, and makes her way cautiously over the stony ground towards her car. She turns and looks up at the sombre grey building with the stark metal cross outlined against the pale blue sky. The place where one life had ended and where two lives have just begun.

A priest in a black robe and dog collar, with a Bible tucked under his arm, passes her. 'Grace and peace, madam,' he says, smiling, his crooked white teeth lighting up his weathered brown face.

'And to you too, Father,' she replies, watching him make his way to a familiar-looking, battered old Land Rover parked under an acacia tree. Its engine splutters to life and the acrid smell of diesel blasts from the exhaust pipe as it jerks away. She watches it disappear down the dusty road and, as they do every day, her thoughts turn to Damien.

Father Damien. It was he who helped her to find her way out of the blackness, the dark hole she had been living in since Michael's death, to find hope in the midst of her despair and to see beauty again in things she no longer noticed. It was he who taught her that she could love again, and that love will be forever buried in her heart.

But a priest belongs to everyone. Except that Damien Donnelly is no longer a priest and Cynthia suspects that he now belongs to someone. Someone very special who stole his heart many years ago.

Serendipity, fate, destiny? she ponders, getting behind the wheel of her Pajero. *I'll take Grace*

References

1. Autumn – John Clare
2. First Love – John Clare
3. Storm at Sea
4. First Love – John Clare
5. Dog Songs – Mary Oliver
6. He Wishes for the Cloths of Heaven –
W B Yeats
7. Isaiah 47:3
8. The Journey – Mary Oliver
9. He Wishes for the Cloths of Heaven –
W B Yeats
10. I know Someone – Mary Oliver
11. The Circle Game – Joni Mitchell
12. Jeremiah 31:15
13. Sons and Lovers – D H Lawrence
14. A Visit from St Nicholas – Clement
Clarke Moore
15. Matthew 6:34
16. The Summer Day – Mary Oliver
17. The Uses of Sorrow – Mary Oliver
18. Wild Geese – Mary Oliver
19. A Thousand Mornings – Mary Oliver
20. Auguries of Innocence – William Blake
21. The Invitation – Oriah Mountain Dreamer
22. When Death Comes – Mary Oliver
23. Heavy – Mary Oliver
24. When Death Comes – Mary Oliver
25. The Coliseum – Lord Byron
26. In Blackwater Woods – Mary Oliver
27. The Sun - Mary Oliver

28. Hamlet – William Shakespeare
29. Cinderella
30. Song of Solomon – The Bible

Printed in Great Britain
by Amazon

22970804R00162